THE
Promise

A Standalone Novel by

C.E. WILSON

Congrats Mark!

C.E. Wilson.

Maggie Munyon, I brought this book back to life because as a friend you inspire me beyond words. I hope to see your books on the shelves one day . . . hopefully right next to mine.

One

60 INCHES / FIVE FEET

*T*HE RING FIT my finger perfectly. The classic silver band with the elegant square diamond was simple, exactly like one I would have chosen myself, and I felt a certain pride knowing that my fiancé understood me so well. He was one of the few people in my life who tried to understand me. The moment was joyous and as we shared kisses, I should have been elated. Me. Lily Evans was now engaged to one of the most beautiful men I had ever seen in my life. And he wanted me, too. It was a moment straight out of a cheesy chick flick, but there was something that tempered my overwhelming happiness.

Erik Larkin had proposed to me on the same day that I was officially diagnosed.

So even though the ring felt right and proper on my finger and didn't clash with the tattoos on my wrist and forearms, the day of his proposal had officially become the best and worst moment of my life.

My boyfriend—*ahem*, I mean fiancé—Erik Larkin smiled gently as he slid the delicate band on my finger and tears came to my eyes in the doctor's office where he had proposed. *So romantic, right?* That was Erik. He knew I didn't care. He knew when the moment was right, and also that the right moment didn't actually exist. When Erik was ready to propose that's exactly what he did. He schmaltzed down to the local jeweler, wagged his dark eyebrows and smiled with a charisma that was best reserved for pharmaceutical reps and grabbed the most expensive ring that I would allow slipped onto to my finger. I liked quality, sure, but quality didn't equal size to me. So despite the fact that the diamond didn't resemble something on a Super Bowl ring, it gleamed with perfection. Erik would call it a 'perfect' diamond because there wasn't a single flaw on the gleaming faceted stone. *God,* how did I end up with such a perfect man? And why did my happiness have to coincide with something so fantastical?

I had dreaded this exact moment for months. *Not the engagement!* The diagnosis.

"Couldn't you wait for something a bit more romantic?" I asked Erik with a teary smile. I hated crying in front of anyone and I hated crying in front of Erik even more. Why? Because he never judged me. He gave me unspoken permission to act human and though I should have been grateful, I only wanted to be stronger. I sucked some snot back into my nose like the graceful princess I was and Erik shook his head with a chuckle . . . which of course turned on the waterworks. How did he manage to do that?

"It's alright," he said, smiling warmly. "So long as you're crying out of happiness and not utmost disgust."

I sucked in another sob. "Shut up. You know why I'm crying, idiot." I didn't tell Erik, but I think he knew that my tears were borne of both happiness, and also fear. We both wondered . . . *how long would the ring fit my finger as well as it did on the day he proposed?*

Perhaps I need to explain. I'm getting ahead of myself and I don't want people to think I'm a whiny, emotional baby who cries over proposals from handsome, witty, sexy Gods like my future hubby.

I was shrinking.

Please don't laugh. It sounds crazy, but it's true. The day Erik proposed I was already short, barely standing five feet tall. It's not that short, but considering I used to be almost six, losing a foot was already enough of a shock to my system.

I had been shrinking for the past few months, and Erik had been kind enough to stay with me. At five feet tall, I already felt like a child sitting next to him, looking more like his daughter than his wife-to-be. Well, other than the fact that Erik and I were polar opposites in regards to physical appearance.

My tattered-on-purpose jeans were loose—even though they came from the junior's department—and it was becoming more difficult to find clothes that didn't make me look younger than I already felt. I never planned on wearing clothes from stores that featured slumped over emo mannequins after the age of twelve, but they fit me better than most other places. Staring down at the whiskered effect across my thighs and the tacky gemstone sewn against the right hip pocket, I realized there were times when I felt less and less human and more like a doll.

Through all of that, as much as I wanted to curse the world, when Erik's light blue eyes stared into mine and he shot me another warm smile, I swear my heart almost burst into a sexy puddle of red blood.

"I couldn't wait another moment to propose to you, Lily. I wanted to do this sooner, but I was so sure you'd run away after the test results came in." He lowered his head, unable to hide his face because of a short, professional cut across his jet black hair. My fiancé the business man. "I don't want to lose you," he whispered, hinting at a future that I didn't want to accept.

"You are going to lose me." My voice cracked as I leaned over the chair and cupped his warm and scruffy cheek into my palm. Despite styled hair, my man needed a shave. I'd been with enough bad boys. I loved that Erik was professional and clean shaven. I spared him a sad smile as I realized how quickly I could lose all of this. *Lose all of him.* "One way or another, things are going to change."

The doctor cleared his throat, eyes wet, touched by the strange scene that unfolded before him. In his albeit few years of practicing medicine he had never heard of anything like my case. No doctor had.

Dr. Russel—Mark, as we knew him—was a friend of Erik's family and close to our age. After insistent begging from Erik and his parents, he decided to step in as, not only a medical professional, but also a protector. At first he didn't want to believe, and I couldn't say that I blamed him. But when he saw the numbers changing, the numbers diminishing week-by-week, day-by-day, he realized that he couldn't bluster and chortle at the results any longer—especially when his friend was hurting. So despite his initial reservations about me, he agreed to help out in any way he could and keep all medical information confidential. I couldn't shake the feeling that Mark didn't want Erik to see me spend the rest of my life as a circus freak, shrinking at an uncontrollable rate with no end in sight, so as his friend, he swallowed his reservations and did the best he could. Dealing with me was a risk to his name, pedigree and professional reputation, but Erik didn't leave him with much of a choice.

Mark could probably easily remember when we first met. I had been tall, almost as tall as Erik. Not anymore. Mark wasn't sure why it was happening, or when it would stop, but he promised to do everything in his power to keep our secret for my sake and Erik's.

"We don't know what the future holds, Lily," Mark said gruffly from behind his desk. He leaned forward, steepling his hands. "This . . . shrinking . . . it could stop at any time."

He was still so uncomfortable saying the word. Shrinking. Shrinking was a subject left for science-fiction and *The Twilight Zone*, not for a man practicing modern medicine. He surveyed us over his knuckles.

"I used to be almost six feet tall," I started off.

"I know, Lily. No one is denying that."

I ignored his pathetic attempt to placate me with calm words and continued to raise my voice. "Now look at me!" I motioned to my body and held out my large platforms shoes that barely poked out from under my too-long jeans.

"Lily . . ." Mark started. "You shouldn't get yourself riled up."

"How about you try to deal with this and not get riled up, huh?" I shouted.

"This could stop at any time."

"How can we know that? You didn't even believe this was happening until a few months ago and now suddenly you're an expert? You're telling me this'll stop? You can't know, Mark! You have nothing to base anything on!" Every action of mine lately reminded me of a child's. I took in a deep breath, afraid that Erik would pluck me up off my chair, settle me in his lap, and run his fingers gently through my dreadlocks.

Thankfully I wasn't that short . . . *yet*.

I glanced up at Erik. His tall, lean body slumped heavily in his chair. Even as a formerly tall woman, I didn't understand how short girls wanted a tall man; I already found Erik a little intimidating. Despite the outward appearance of a professional, his eyes carried heavy bags and his cheeks sunk in slightly. Erik looked as though he existed in black and white while the rest of the world flourished in Technicolor. My diagnosis took as heavy a toll on him as it did on me. My heart bled for him, wondering how he managed to fall and remain in love with me before he leaned in close and kissed my temple. My skin blazed from the brush of his lips. His expensive cologne that reminded me of oranges and freshly mown lawn invaded my nostrils. The tiny ring he had slipped on my finger a few minutes before and that familiar scent took me back to earlier times and happier memories.

"I love you, Lily," he whispered into my black dreadlocks, refusing to let me get caught up in the past. "Nothing will ever change that."

"Not even a few lost inches?" I grumbled.

"Nope."

"Not even a few feet?"

"Come on, Lily. You can't possibly get that much smaller. You're probably not going to change that much."

"I've already lost a foot, Erik. The truth is staring me in the face every morning. And you don't know what else is going to change. Neither of you do."

The day that Erik proposed should have been the happiest day of my life, but because of some impossible illness, it was ruined. I couldn't smile without the future hanging over my ever diminishing body. The future watched me with a smirk. It gave me the man of my dreams—the life I always dreamed of—but it was all temporary. Soon it would all be forgotten and I would become nothing more than Erik's 'little thing' before long.

The thought left me breathless.

Five years ago I fell in love with Erik and him with me, despite all our differences. Where I was dark, Erik was light. His skin was nearly translucent on a sunny day with hair that was a bluish black that he never bothered to style at the time. His vibrant ice blue eyes were a striking contrast to his jet black hair. He knew how to dress and I swear on my life, I never thought I would fall in love with a man who wore a peacoat and penny loafers.

Erik came from a good family.

I didn't.

I grew up with a single mother who put me up for adoption when I was eleven. *Yes, eleven.* I could remember her when I wanted to, but most of my memories were of the foster homes I grew up in until I was eighteen. Some were good and some were bad. I acted out in the bad ones, regrettably covering both my arms with tattoos and piercing my nose and eyebrows several times. I let my dark hair grow out into messy dreadlocks and I smoked like a chimney which caused grey circles to form under the delicate skin of my hazel eyes. I didn't care much about anything during my teenage years, but no one did.

What did it matter if I got lung cancer?

If my own mother didn't want me, who would?

I made so many poor decisions when I was younger and I would never have the chance to find out if one of them led me to the doctor's office that day. What if it was just one extra cigarette? What if I had quit smoking sooner? What if I forgot to check one needle to make sure it was pure before I got tattooed or pierced? What if? I could ask myself all these questions until I was dead and I would never know the answers. The answers didn't even matter. Not really. The only question I had lately was, am I actually shrinking?

And somehow, despite reality, the answer was yes.

I WAS NINETEEN WHEN ERIK and I first met.

He was a smartass college student and I was just a smartass.

I had no way to pay for an endeavor such as post high-school education and besides, my grades were so poor that I barely got my diploma. I think my gym teacher Ms. Meyers and my Physics teacher Mr. Michaels were willing to pass me just to get me the hell out their building. I could remember spending many a days and nights studying my ass out just to get out of that place . . . wait, what? No, I'm kidding. I never studied. I was the kid who just showed up with a thermos filled with juice that smelled like nail polish remover and considered the day a success if I made it through without a fight. I wasn't an aggressive kid, but people always assumed the worst in me when they found out I came from the foster care system. They'd take one look at my hand-me-down black skinny jeans, sleeveless plaid shirt and the cigarette between my lips and paint me as a bad seed. I didn't help change peoples' minds. I hated homework, studying, tests, gym, writing, computers, authority figures, non-authority figures, my classmates, the swim team, the drama weirdos, the band nuts, the preppies, the sportos, the nerds, the freaks . . . wait, that's *The Breakfast Club*. Either way, for some reason high school and I didn't get along.

But I *did* graduate. Not that anyone showed up. The only people who probably cheered when I went up to take my diploma were the guidance counselor and the Nazi lookalike who ran in-school suspension in a basement that smelled like snotty tissues and broken pens. Yay.

And somehow . . . through all of our differences in upbringing, Erik and I both ended up working at the same restaurant near a small, private university.

Erik Larkin's presence was a breath of fresh air compared to the stale stench of American fare greasy spoon 'cooking' that filled the air at American Wake. Every day he would stride into the tacky place like he owned it with several textbooks in his slim, sturdy arms and dump them on the counter. He'd complain about one professor and the next. Sometimes, he'd even ask me for help on assignments. I'd light up like a damn Christmas tree when those ice blue eyes sought out mine even though most of the time I didn't have the slightest idea what he was asking me or talking about. After a while, I started to listen. I learned. Erik held my attention in a way that my high school teachers only dreamt about. He looked at me as though I was the only person in the world. God, I wanted him, but despite his kindness and warmth he was still so out of my league.

It didn't take a fool to understand that he came from a good family. He was always well-dressed, a new version of Patrick Bateman . . . minus the whole *American Psycho* thing. He'd come in with a familiar white and green coffee cup as though it was glued to his hand and his cologne always mixed with coffee beans and caramel. It was a deadly combination with his sky blue eyes and black hair. I found myself trying to improve my image on the days we'd work together. I'd seen him in dark blue jeans and henleys that strained to contain his slim, but strong chest. I saw his Calvin Klein jacket stretch in the back between his shoulders where he was the most built. And when he was seated, I could always tell that his socks didn't match despite inwardly calculating the cost of his Dr. Martens. I felt like such a homeless bum next to him that after while . . . and it became clear that he wasn't leaving any time soon, I was more careful about covering my tattooed arms with long-sleeved undershirts. I even let a few of my piercings close because he didn't have a single one and I assumed the girls he dated probably didn't have any either—other than maybe a pair of half-carat diamond studs.

Erik started paying more attention to me. Talking to me longer. Finding excuses to stay and chat while he tugged on that Calvin Klein jacket and scuffed his black Dr. Martens into the cheap flooring at The Wake. I kept making small adjustments in hopes that this would continue. I pulled my dreads into high, tight ponytails to reveal my face. Not the best face in the world, but a decent face. Sharp, high cheekbones and thick natural lashes that one of my foster moms hated. My eyes were a shocking shade of hazel which always made me wonder just what my real dad looked like. I stopped once at a drugstore and bought a pale pink gloss that matched my lips. More attention. More smiles.

They turned flirtatious. I kept going despite knowing the fact that a guy like Erik Larkin would never really give me the time of day outside work. I left my cigarettes in the car on the days I knew he would be there. He always smelled so good—like coffee and cream, and citrus and grass—so I had to wonder if he could smell me as well. I wanted to smell good. I found a cheap perfume in the clearance bin at the same drugstore I bought the gloss at. Something with coconuts.

I knew Erik noticed the effort I had made to look 'clean myself up' when he was around, but I couldn't help wondering how much he cared. The changes I made weren't just good for him, but for me as well. Since I didn't smoke as much, I didn't sneak out so much for breaks so I wasn't getting stiffed out of tips. My boss was happy with this. Some of the other guys at work started to notice me as well. I stopped eating so much junk food so my body turned leaner. One guy said I had a sexy collarbone. I wondered if Erik thought the same thing. I got asked out on a few dates by guys in and out of the restaurant after the changes, but I couldn't bring myself to accept.

I just wanted confirmation that there was *no way* I could date a guy like Erik.

I also wanted more than jokes about *The Simpsons* and statements that I really was 'different from other girls'. What did that even mean? Was that a good thing or a bad thing? Based on his facial expression it had to be good, but how right could my conclusion be? It wasn't like I was smart.

Weeks rolled into months and Erik was still around. Still smiling. Still working the same shifts I did if someone called out. I started looking forward to going to work more often. I asked for more shifts. *His shifts.* I saw him four or five days a week. He was a fixture in my life, surely I was a fixture in his by now? Did he think about me the same way I thought about him? Stupid girly daydreams about going to the movies and laughing in the car during road trips? Things I never wanted to do before, I suddenly was dying to try. With him. I wanted to buy some girly movies and indulge, but I couldn't bring myself to do so. My imagination was free, after all.

Whether it was him coming in from the parking lot, walking across the street to grab the working shift milkshakes, or standing outside to talk with a friend from college who stopped by, I'd watch Erik. Here I am calling him Patrick Bateman, when I guess I'm the one who's a bit psycho. Erik had this ability to practically glide across a floor no matter where he was or what surrounded him. Whether he was in a sweater, jacket, henley or t-shirt with some 80s band, every movement was fluid. I often found myself checking out his shoulders when he'd hunch over to talk to people. The strain of the fabric between his shoulder blades was such a turn on for some reason. And to top it off Erik Larkin was tall. Not surprising, right? Who doesn't find tall guys sexy, but it was rare for me to find someone so attractive who was also taller than me. As I stood nearly six feet tall, I was used to being an intimidating sight for most guys, but Erik made me feel like a delicate girly girl from the start. I remember the way he used to come up behind me at work and whisper something about a customer in my ear. How his breath would set my cheeks on fire and send tingles in my belly and places just a slight bit lower. I remembered his large hands resting next to mine when we were waiting for orders to come up. His fingernails were always clean and I bet they smelled like coffee beans.

Sometimes he would catch me staring at him like an idiot.

"What are you looking at, Lils?" he'd ask.

God. I loved when he said my name and I loved it even more that he had a little nickname for me. That had to mean something. *Lils.* No one ever called me that before because few people took the time to get to know me. Lily wasn't exactly a name that matched my outward appearance. I probably should have had a name like Kelly or Morgan or Erica. Something strong and less . . . flowery.

"Lils?" he'd try again, probably wondering if I was slow.

I would turn to take in his face and shake my head, trying not to get lost in those huge, ice blue eyes. It wasn't right for a man to be so damn pretty, masculine, and intense at the same time. Who was this guy, Dean—freakin'—Winchester?

"It's nothing," I would answer shyly, taking my order before he could noticed my red cheeks. The butterflies in my lower belly were violent and if he touched me I worried I'd melt into the floor into a greasy purple, pink and red puddle shaped like a heart. I just felt so girly around him and poor guy, he probably didn't have the slightest clue as to why I acted so strangely around him. I'd sneak a gaze over my shoulder at him before I disappeared into the serving room, wondering if he was looking at me too. Usually, he was whispering with the younger cook who worked in the back.

I wanted to know what they talked about.

More weeks passed by and because of my complete change in attitude I was eventually promoted to assistant manager at American Wake. Probably because my boss, Lukas knew I wasn't going to leave any time soon for college or a better job opportunity. I was fine with it. I asked Lukas if I could bartend over the weekends and he said okay. In fact, the middle-aged man seemed pleased. Rarely did his dark brown eyes reach anything better than 'not unhappy'. I was floored. Maybe one day he'd even smile.

In the course of a few months, life didn't seem so terrible. In fact, it seemed down right awesome. I had a decent job, made decent money and led a decent life. Cigarettes were a treat at the end of a shitty work day, not a ten-times-a-day indulgence. With no more tattoos or piercings I had a little extra spending money. Sometimes I'd sneak into a bookstore and browse some of the books Erik brought to work, wondering what got his mind working—what he thought about during his breaks. Usually I'd end up with a teen drama manga instead of *War and Peace*, but I made the effort. I felt like I wasn't an idiot. Maybe . . . I was even smart. Special, even.

And then my world exploded.

On a particularly dreary night I went out to my car after a long shift. Erik had left an hour before so I undid my ponytail and let my dreads wildly fall around my neck, shoulder, and back. I pulled off my starchy white shirt in the parking lot and stood in my tight grey halter, rubbing my colorful arms. I really had overdone it as a teenager, and though I had no plans to get anything new, I could never imagine getting rid of my tattoos. They were a part of my identity and, so long as I kept them covered as an assistant manager, they didn't seem to cause me any problems at the restaurant.

Lukas was actually downright cool with my tats, showing me a few of his one day when he let his guard down. But that wasn't that night. Lukas was a jackassy mess earlier and because of his temper, I dropped a few plates in the kitchen, further infuriating him. But the night was over and the plates weren't going to be taken from my check after a heartfelt promise to work the dreaded Sunday evening shift which was filled with no one other than early bird old grannies and churchgoers hoping to 'cut loose' before going back to work on Monday. They were all lousy tippers.

I let out a sigh of relief knowing the day was over and reached into my glove compartment, desperate for my half-empty pack of cigarettes and lit one. It had been a long night. I needed this. I leaned against my car, and the cool breeze teased my shoulders before I exhaled a thin plume of smoke into the air. My lungs burned because they weren't as used to the nicotine. I thought about stubbing it out and heading back to my dreary one bedroom apartment when a voice startled me from behind, but not because of lack of familiarity.

"So you *are* still smoking."

"Erik!" I spun around as my heart quickened its pace.

There weren't many cars left in the lot and Erik stood only a few spaces away, with a gentle frown on his face. He needed to shave. Or maybe he didn't. The stubble looked good on him despite the frown. He lifted his hand in an awkward greeting and for a few moments, my mouth failed to articulate.

"What are you still doing here?" I finally got out. I tried to hide my cigarette by my side but there wasn't really a point. He caught me. He probably hadn't seen me smoke in months. I remained defensive and surprised as he walked towards me. Butterflies fluttered. "I thought . . . I thought you were done for the night." *Smooth.*

He shrugged. "I was . . . but . . ."

I dared to glance up. "But . . ."

He laughed awkwardly, rubbing the back of his neck. I swear his eyes scanned the parking lot. Was he waiting for someone? Was I making this more awkward for him than it was for me? Was such a thing even possible?

"I was waiting for you."

The cigarette leapt from my fingers as my hand jerked. I quickly stomped it out to make it look intentional but my expression must have betrayed my shock.

"Waiting for me?" My heart pounded heavily in my ears and color rushed up to my cheeks. Our eyes hadn't met yet and it was probably for the best. "Why? Did you want to ask me to cover a shift?"

He shook his head with his attention on the ground. "Not exactly."

"Oh. So then . . . uh . . . what for?"

He took a couple lazy steps over and stopped a few feet in front of me. Could he feel my heart pounding? Could he smell the cigarette on my breath as I struggled to breathe? Tugging oh-so-sexily at the end of my shirt and focusing on my shoes, I waited as patiently as I could for him to answer when in reality, my mind raced.

Erik Larkin. Erik Larkin here to see me. Didn't say what for. Not a bad sign. Maybe a good sign.

"I didn't borrow a book from you, did I?" I tried.

"No, no. Nothing like that." He sounded nervous as we both continued to stare at our feet. He at his expensive black Dr. Martens, and me at my cheap sneakers designed to look like Converse sneakers that weren't. "And if you did . . . you uh . . . you can keep it."

"Thanks?" I couldn't even begin to think about how awkward my voice must have sounded. "So if you're not here to ask me about a shift . . . or a book . . . what . . . what are you here for?"

Another shrug. He was wearing my favorite Calvin Klein jacket. The one I bet smelled like him—coffee and cream and grass and oranges. I wanted to bury myself in his chest and find out if that coat smelled as good as he did, but he spoke again, breaking my train of thought.

"I don't really know."

I arched a brow. "You don't know?"

"All I know is that I wanted to see you."

He shifted awkwardly and I dared to lift my chin. Intense blue eyes bore into mine. *Shit.* They widened momentarily as he snuck in a once over. I felt naked under his steel gaze. Damn. He made me feel so small. He held his gaze longer than he ever did when we were on the clock. I was the first to try focusing on the flickering lights of a drive-thru window, willing my cheeks to cool down and match the late evening air.

"You look really different outside of work."

Self-consciously my hand darted up to my Medusa-like hair. "Geezus, I probably look like shit—"

"No, it's fine," Erik said quickly, taking a step forward.

My attention darted upward and we locked eyes. Heat rushed to my cheeks, but I swear the tips of his ears turned pink. With such pale skin, it was almost impossible to hide. When he realized how close we were, he quickly stuffed his hands into his pockets and rocked back on his heels. He coughed awkwardly. God. Everything was awkward.

"I mean . . . it looks cool."

I tried to remain neutral. "Thanks."

He must have taken my neutrality for being defensive because his voice turned rushed again. "I know you have to wear it up for work, but I really like it this way too. I really like it."

He really likes it. I blushed. "Oh . . . well thanks. Again."

His eyes narrowed, tracing down my now-exposed arms and his eyebrows rose sky high. "And those!" He exclaimed with interest. "I've heard about them, and I thought I saw them once or twice, but . . . *wow.*"

My attention drifted down to what held his captive. So he hadn't gotten a good look at my tattoos until now. I didn't know what I wanted to cover first, my hair or my arms. I thought about grabbing my shirt again and turned to open my car door.

"Hey, it's okay," he chuckled, as though he knew exactly what I was up to. "I don't have a problem with them. I didn't know that you had so many."

He stepped closer and I craned my neck to gaze up at him. Despite being a rich, pretty boy, he was still pretty intimidating. His hand reached towards my arm and I instinctively pulled away.

"I'm sorry, I only wanted to get a better look. You can't really show them at work, so . . ." he trailed off and reached for me. "Is it okay?"

"Oh . . . uh sure." I held my arm out to him and my skin caught fire under his touch as he took one of my arms gently in his hand.

"These are amazing, Lily." He inspected them closely as I

struggled to breathe. "And you're so young . . . when did you get all of these?"

"Too young," I said with a trace of embarrassment. "I was a messed up kid."

He chuckled as he spotted some old school Nintendo characters. "You're a gamer?"

I pulled my arm away. "Not really. Like I said, I was young. I had some friends who did them for free. All clean and legit, but I kind of let them do whatever they want."

"I see."

He straightened up and the moonlight struck his face. I lost my breath for a moment just watching him.

"So which one is your favorite?" He glanced awkwardly around the parking lot.

I felt self-conscious about showing him a tattoo that actually meant something to me. It was kind of silly, but the placement of it . . . I wasn't sure. "There is one that I really like," I whispered almost to myself.

His dark eyebrows shot up. "Really? Which one?"

"Um, it's not on my arms. It's somewhere else."

The corner of his mouth quirked upward. "Oh?"

"Uh, yeah," I tugged on my shirt like a child does when hiding something. "It's on my stomach."

"Man, you are hard core," he said with a light laugh. "I'm kidding though, Lils. Let me see it."

I pressed my lips into a thin line, trying not to smile like an idiot every time he said my name. "You really want to?"

He paused with a smile. "Hmm . . . do I want to see a beautiful woman pull up her shirt and show me a piece of art on her body that means something to her? Do I want the chance to learn more about the woman who absolutely fascinates me every time I see her?" He nodded. "Show me."

I tried to play it cool, but his interest in me was intoxicating.

I didn't often speak to him, but as he spoke those few sentences I think I fell for him even more. He found me beautiful? He didn't mind my tattoos? He wanted to learn more about me? I fascinated him? My mind reeled as I carefully pulled up my top, exposing the thin strip of skin from the top of my pants to my belly button. This particular tattoo didn't have a friend in sight. I had a few on my legs and a few on my shoulders, but the tattoo on my stomach stood alone. It was artless, and I think Erik was surprised by the simplicity of this symbol that mattered so much to me. I sucked in my stomach so he wouldn't see that I ate about twelve mozzarella sticks for dinner, but his eyes only seemed to focus on the art.

"A book?" He crouched down, placing his hands on his thighs and narrowing his eyes.

"Not just any book, it was a book that Mom left with me when she dropped me off at the orphanage."

His eyebrow arched. "No title?"

"Can't remember the title. I only remember the book itself."

"All those times you asked me about what books I was reading, you never mentioned that you liked to read."

I tried not to think about how close his face was to my exposed skin. "I don't have a lot of spare money, but I love to get my hands on a good book, especially manga. Goodwill usually has the best selection that I can afford."

He laughed, probably having never even set foot inside a Goodwill, and was gracious enough not to point that out. "I like to get my hands on good books too."

I nearly fainted when he began to reach towards the open book on my stomach. I clenched my eyes shut as his fingertips touched the skin, tracing up and down the lines of the blank cover.

"Sorry, but I've been waiting a long time for a chance to talk to you like this."

"Really?" I breathed out.

He nodded, lowered his hand and slowly rose up back into a standing position. "Yes."

He was so close that I could almost touch my forehead to his chin, but instead I stared up at him with wide eyes. *Was this really happening? Was I dreaming?*

It felt real.

"Lily," he started, "do you want to . . . go out sometime?"

"Go . . . out?" Ugh, I probably sounded like such an idiot.

"Yeah . . . uh. With me."

I swallowed. "Are you . . . are you asking me out on a date?"

"It certainly appears that way doesn't it?" Erik said, blushing. "I mean, I know I'm probably not your type but . . ."

"What makes you say that?"

He shrugged. "I dunno. You kind of have this whole badass thing going on. I probably seem like just another rich brat to you, but I can't help it. I dunno . . . I'm interested in you."

"Interested in me?" I couldn't believe what I was hearing. It didn't seem possible. But it was. I couldn't help myself. Before I could think about it, I reached out and grabbed his face, pulling his lips to mine. He tasted like . . ."Did you eat onion rings?" I joked, breathlessly.

"Technically they were onion fries," he said sheepishly. He went on to shrug with a smirk on his features. "So I take your reaction means yes?"

I nodded, pulling him in for another kiss. "Damn right," I whispered.

FIVE YEARS HAD PASSED SINCE that day, and the memory still gave me goosebumps. I jerked in surprise when I realized Erik was patting me gently on the back. Slightly startled out of my reverie, I still didn't want to let fear show on my face. Fear of not only what was happening to me; but also of losing something I wanted to keep so badly. I was already enough of a burden for him—it had taken me years to win over his father—and now I was becoming even more of a burden.

"Should we celebrate?" he suggested.

"Celebrate what?" I mumbled. "Celebrate the fact that I'm a freak, or the fact that you're engaged to a freak?"

"You're not a freak," Erik said firmly. "This will stop. Right, Mark?"

"This could stop today for all we know," Mark answered hopefully, but his eyes revealed he didn't believe his own words.

"Not a freak, huh? So how tall am I?" I asked Mark sharply, picking up on the fact that he wasn't being completely honest. I stood up and Erik quickly followed suit. His hands rested on my shoulders, and I quickly jerked out of his grasp so I could focus on Mark.

"W-what . . . what does that matter?" Mark asked and glimpsed towards my fiancé, who tried to gently move me out of his office. Even though I barely reached his armpit, I stood firm.

"How tall am I? You measured me this morning; I was five feet even last week. How tall?"

"Lily, let's get some dinner . . ." Erik tried, but I pulled away.

"How tall, dammit?" I shouted at Mark.

He lowered his eyes for a moment, resting his hands on his desk. Doctor's hands. Not a callous or a scar on a single finger or knuckle. "4' 10 ½"," Mark answered.

Erik and I simultaneously sucked in a gasp.

Still shrinking.

"I see."

"Lily . . ." Mark tried.

With slumped shoulders, I finally allowed Erik to lead me out of the office.

"Can't wait to sit in that booster seat." I really didn't

understand how short women did it. I missed being almost six feet tall. At just shy of five feet, the world was starting to become a pretty scary place. Bodies loomed in all directions, and even with platform shoes I was shorter than almost everyone I encountered. A girl brushed past me in the office, seeming like a giant and probably still in middle school. I don't think she even registered in my fiancé's mind.

"Lily, you're not *that* short." He shut the door behind us. "You're just a little shorter than the average American woman."

"Alright, Mr. *National Geographic.* You would have never even glanced my way if I was five feet tall when we first met," I muttered. I tried to look assertive as I walked down the halls with Erik trailing behind me a few feet, probably nervous that I would snap at him.

I pressed the elevator button, got in and punched the lobby button quickly, sealing the two of us in the confined space before someone else could come in and remind me of this strange and horrible situation. I regarded the underside of Erik's chin through my lashes. He was so tall already, and he would only continue to get larger unless this stopped. The thought took my breath away. I didn't want my fiancé to become a giant in my eyes. I didn't want this.

Erik remained silent during the elevator ride with his eyebrows knotted close together.

"Are you kidding me?" He finally blurted out as we both walked through the door and into the parking lot. "I would have looked at you if you were wearing a potato sack."

I flushed. "Ten minutes and that's the best you've got?" I said angrily. "That fancy college you graduated from really taught you how to communicate." I continued to try to get into the car but before I could open the passenger side he stepped in front of me. Leaning against the door, he lowered his chin to lock his eyes on mine.

"Lily," he said in a low voice, using his finger to lift my chin up toward his. I tried to pull away but he wrapped both of his hands around my cheeks and lowered his face. Our noses touched and I was flooded with spicy citrus. "Don't you remember how I used to trip myself up trying to talk to you? How stupid I sounded?"

Despite my mood, I couldn't help grinning as the memories came flooding back. "I can't believe I ever thought you were cool. You were such a dork."

His crooked smile appeared. "And I still am. And now I'm your dork fiancé."

What remained of my anger evaporated, but I had to think about our future and how everything was changing so drastically. "Are you sure you really want to do this?"

"What? Go out to dinner? Of course I do, I'm starving."

I nudged him with my elbow. "You know that's not what I mean. Are you sure you want to do this . . . with me, I mean? You don't have to stick around if you—"

"Don't say stupid things," he said gruffly. "I just proposed to you and you're still worried I'm gonna up and leave you?"

I shrugged, feeling stupid for having already forgotten the ring he slid onto my finger. "I still don't get what you see in me."

He leaned in and kissed me softly. "It must be because of how badass you are," he laughed.

"Shut up," I said, smiling. "Why do you have to make fun of me all the time?"

He shrugged and playfully pinched my cheek. "Why do you have to make fun of yourself all the time? I swear, Lils, you will never be able to see yourself the way I do." Dropping his arm, he reached down and took my hand.

I stared at the simple white gold band and tiny square diamond. He could have given me something gaudier, but that wouldn't have made me happier. And he knew that. It made the ring so much more special.

"It really is beautiful," I said, holding my hand up to the sun. "More than I deserve."

"You deserve to be happy, goofball. I promise that I will try to keep you happy, and I hope I can be the one that you'll stay with until . . ."

"Until the end?" I answered grimly.

Hopelessness chose to fall over me like a tidal wave at that exact moment. Why was this happening? Things like this weren't supposed to happen! People just don't wake up one day and start shrinking! I reached out and grabbed Erik's polo.

"I don't want this!" I screamed into his chest as he hunched over to wrap his arms around my waist. "I don't want to shrink into nothing!"

"You're not going to."

"I mean, what the hell? What the hell is going to happen to me, Erik?"

"Shh . . . come on, Lils." Erik lightly ran his long fingers through my dreads all the way down to the scalp. "You're not going to shrink into nothing. You're being crazy."

"The height charts say otherwise. I can't do this. I can't deal with it."

"You won't have to deal with it. Not alone, at least."

My voice cracked. "I don't want you to have to deal with this either. I want to wake up and for this all to be one messed up dream from a night of too much drinking."

"That's very *Twilight Zone*," Erik said calmly.

"Seriously," I groaned. "I don't want this."

"I know."

His lips touched the top of my head. "Four foot, ten inches, Erik."

"And a half," he added. "Let's try and be positive."

I couldn't help snorting into his shirt. "Easy for you to say, you're not the one shrinking."

"I won't pretend to understand what you're going through, but I will be there all the way. You're my fiancé, and by the end of this week . . ." he paused for a moment. "I plan on making you my wife. If you'll give me the honor."

This caught me off-guard. He actually wanted to marry me? I thought that by putting a ring on my finger he was doing the right thing. But he wanted me to be his wife . . . his real wife . . . forever? I stared up at him with wide eyes. "Really?"

"Why are you so shocked with a ring on your finger? Yes, really. Now can we please go celebrate?" he said in an almost playful, whiny tone.

It was hard not to smile when he regarded me with those light blue eyes. They hypnotized me as they always had, and they kept me from falling into a depression now. He guided me by the hand into the passenger seat and closed the door.

I glimpsed around my surroundings. Erik's stereo and the MP3 player in the cup holder. Discarded coffee cups on the floor and in the back. How long would it be before I would require his help to get into a car? To change the radio from another one of his awful classic rock tunes to something with a bit more soul? Would I shrink so much that I wouldn't be able to move around our home? To drive my car? Would I still be able to keep my independence if I got much smaller? How much smaller could I possibly get?

As Erik settled into the driver's seat, I couldn't help staring at his huge hands gripping the steering wheel. How long would this go on? People get smaller in old age, yes, but this couldn't go on for much longer.

People didn't just start shrinking. It didn't happen. Or rather, it shouldn't happen.

"Lils?" Erik asked, pulling me from my ever wandering thoughts. "You okay?"

I steeled my jaw. I wouldn't be weak. "Yeah, babe," I said softly before turning to focus on the window. "I'm gonna be okay."

Two

54 Inches / 4 feet, 6 Inches

I BROWSED THROUGH the clothes at Double Zero, a trendy store that accommodated insanely teensy girls. I would have never set foot in a store like this normally, but I was having a difficult enough time finding clothes that fit me at all, let alone that fit well. I wasn't built like most women or teenagers who were my height; my entire body seemed to be shrinking proportionally. From a distance I probably looked like a very petite teenager. I could still pass for an adult, a very short adult . . . but barely.

"Sweetie, can I help you with anything?" A syrupy sweet voice cooed from behind me.

I turned around and a sales clerk stood there with an expression that I couldn't decipher. Her fire-engine hair was incredibly long and sleek and her make-up probably took four hours just to look like she wasn't wearing any. The clothing at Double Zero probably fit her perfectly.

My mind reeled as I tried to glance past the red head. Erik said he was running to get a coffee and now I must have looked like a child who needed their mother.

"I'm fine, thank you." I promptly turned my attention back towards the racks and shuffled through the hangers.

"You know, we have some . . . uh . . . more petite clothing in the back," Fire Engine offered carefully.

"More petite than this?"

She nodded, which gracefully moved some strands into her green eyes. "Yes. We here at Double Zero understand that not every child . . ." she trailed off and I glared at her. Somehow she caught the hint. "I mean woman, has been blessed with curves. Some women need the right clothing to bring out their shape."

With the way I was going, it probably made more sense to buy something that fit snugly rather than loosely.

"Here's your coffee, Lils." Erik's voice was a breath of much needed air from behind as he handed me a familiar cup.

"Thank hell you're back," I muttered before taking a sip.

"I was telling your friend about the department we set up in the back," Fire Engine explained to Erik with that overly sweet and sticky smile. She seemed to be quite proud of herself as she smoothed down her slinky black top and fixed Erik with a smirk. "I think she'll find exactly what she's looking for."

Erik glanced over her head and then down at me. "That's the children's department," he said, unsure whether to frown or laugh.

I glared up at the clerk with cheeks the color that matched her hair. "Children's department?"

She held up her hands and started to bluster, losing that damn smirk. "Well . . . um yes. I guess that I assumed . . ."

"You assumed what?"

"I'm sorry, miss." She had the nerve to look towards Erik for help. "I'm sure I'm not the first."

"You're not," Erik said patiently. He took a sip from his cup and I longed to see Erik's face, but I didn't want to take my glaring expression away from the clerk. "It's been happening a lot lately. Please excuse my wife."

"Your wife?" she blurted, turning to me. "But you're . . ."

"I'm what? Short? I'm almost five feet tall in these heels," I grumped.

"I'm sorry. I didn't know." Fire Engine's face was almost as red as mine was.

Erik began waving her off. "Just go, we'll be fine from here."

"Well, my name is Dallas if you need any help," she tried.

"That name is fitting," I muttered under my breath.

"We'll be fine," Erik said plainly.

The girl scurried away before I could get in any more words. If she caught my cutting remark about her porn star name, she didn't bother to point it out. Once out of sight, Erik put his hand on my shoulder and tugged me into his chest. His navy sweater was soft against my cheek.

"Are you okay? Sorry, I keep forgetting that people may mistake you for a child."

"I'm not a damn kid though!" I couldn't help whining into sweater fabric. "If they would actually take the time to look at my face . . . *and these!*" I shouted out, lifting my arms. "What child has sleeve tats?"

"She must not have noticed." He pressed his lips together. "Or maybe . . ."

"Maybe what?" I pulled away completely and stared up at him.

"Maybe that's the reason she approached you in the first place."

"But that . . . oh, dammit." I scrunched up my nose. Made sense. Fire Engine Dallas probably thought I was a no-good kid trying to steal a five dollar tee. "Still . . . she shouldn't have pointed me towards the kid's department. That's as bad as sending a fat woman to the maternity section. If she keeps making mistakes like that, someone's gonna kick her ass."

"Someone . . . like you?"

I smiled. "Maybe."

"That's my Lily alright—a badass kid up to no good!" Erik laughed and pulled me back up against him. It was hard not to wilt under his touch as his chin settled just a few inches above my head.

"Shut up, you," I laughed. "You're making things worse."

He glanced down. "Oh. How's that?"

"They think I'm a kid," I began.

"Uh-huh."

"And you most certainly do not look like a child."

"Still following."

"And now you're wrapping your arms around me in a children's clothing store."

"I believe the term is 'young ladies,'" Erik corrected. "So what?"

"People are going to think you are a pervert . . . or have a fetish."

His face dropped. "Are you serious? Lily, for God's sake, you're not that short! No one's going to think I have a fetish." He smirked. "I'm not you after all, Ms. I'm-Gonna-Read-*The Borrowers*-Ten-Thousand-Times."

"Hey!" I punched him in the arm. "*The Borrowers* is a classic."

"Of course, of course. I've often heard people refer to it as the equal of *To Kill a Mockingbird*," he mocked. He began to browse the racks behind him before his blue eyes lit up. "Tell me, my dear Lily." He pulled out a lacy lingerie set from the racks. "Does this mean I have a fetish?"

"They shouldn't have those here!" I squeaked as Erik put the hanger back. "Stop. Just stop now. We're leaving."

His full lower lip puckered out and his eyes widened. "Oh,

come on. We were just getting to the good stuff."

"There will be no good stuff if you don't get going," I said and began trying to push him. "Damn! I miss being tall. This used to be a lot easier."

"Sorry Lils, but I'm a bit bigger than you now. You can't push me around like you used to."

"You're right!" I grunted in defeat. "Can we please go now?"

"Come on," Erik said with a glint in his eye. "Why don't we get one of those hot numbers so I can see your boobs? Who knows if you'll be able to wear stuff like this again?"

I froze up. "That's really not funny," I muttered and turned away. "Let's go."

"What's not funny about it?" Erik asked, quickly catching up to follow me.

"Making jokes like that. Erik. It's not funny."

I headed straight for the exit. I needed to get out of Double Zero. The entire place was suffocating. The smell of cheap perfume, my own coffee, and cheap fabric. It was too much. Fire Engine lifted her head as I swept past, and merely clucked her tongue and smiled at another woman who entered the store.

"Wait, Lily!" Erik stopped me and grabbed my arm once we were out of the store. "What's wrong? What did I say?"

"That joke. I didn't appreciate it."

"Hey, I'm sorry—"

"Let's go get something to eat, okay?"

"Sure. Whatever you want, but what's wrong?"

"You think I like knowing that I might never be able to wear things like this again?" I mumbled and motioned towards my current outfit. "I already feel ridiculous, and when you say things like that, I dunno, Erik. It really upsets me."

He blinked, the realization finally coming to him. "Oh. I'm sorry."

"I don't need you to say, sorry. I need you to understand not to say those things. Ugh, I hate dealing with feelings, okay? I don't want to get into this at the mall of all places. Just, please, can you imagine what this feels like?"

He shook his head. "I want to understand—"

"You can't."

"I can't."

I took a sip of my coffee and grabbed Erik's hand. "I'm sorry, babe. I don't mean to be so salty."

"No, you're right. That was pretty stupid of me to say, wasn't it?"

"You didn't mean it."

"Well . . . I meant some of it. I did want to see your boobs."

"You're such a pervert." I rolled my eyes.

"It's not being a pervert if it's about my wife." His face grew suddenly serious. "Still, I shouldn't have made that crack about not being able to see you in stuff like that. Hot tits or not."

"You shouldn't have."

"Just the same, Lily, sometimes I just want us to pretend things are okay."

"Pretend," I muttered.

"I know. That makes me a horrible person. But every time I actually think about what is happening to you, I feel like I can't breathe."

"Yeah . . . I felt the same way just now."

"When I made that stupid joke?"

I frowned. "I didn't mean to take you so seriously."

He smacked his forehead. "Dammit, Lils. Why do I always say such stupid stuff around you?"

"You don't say stupid stuff . . . you're just stupid," I said, trying to lighten the mood—desperate to lighten it.

He finally cracked a smile. "But I don't mean it."

I shrugged. "Most of the time."

"Hey, I don't mean it. I'm just hopelessly stupid around

you . . ." He lowered his face towards mine and started to cover my neck and collarbone with kisses. Right outside Double Zero was probably not the best place considering the high traffic of high school girls and their horny boyfriends, but Erik didn't stop. I loved him for that, but that didn't make me any less embarrassed.

"Erik!" I squeaked, trying not to get caught up in his passion. He just made it so hard. "We're in a damn mall! And I can feel that, you know!"

"Can I crack a joke?" he said huskily into my jaw.

"No. You can get that off me. Seriously, people are staring, you idiot."

He kissed my neck. "Pleeeease?"

"Will it piss me off?"

He kissed me tenderly. "Probably."

"Oh, go ahead, you big idiot."

He chuckled, kissing me harder. "If you're saying you look like a teenager and we just came out of a teenager's store . . . don't teenagers make out in malls?"

"We're not teenagers," I breathed as his stubble scratched the thin skin over my throat.

"No, but you look like one."

"Har, har." His lips made contact. "Yeah, but you don't. Old man."

"So I'm a pervert. I'm cool with that."

"Yeah, I can tell you're cool with it! You really are disgusting, babe." I laughed and wrapped my arms around his neck. Glancing around his arm, passerbys stared, probably trying to figure the two of us out. Erik and I making out must have been a strange sight. A man almost six and a half feet tall, making out with a woman two feet shorter. I chuckled and tried to imagine how I would feel if I were the one seeing it.

Once Erik finally calmed himself down, he pushed some of my dreads aside so he could whisper into my ear. "You miss your job yet? Do you miss the girls?"

"Do you?"

"Hell no, but I was never there for the long haul. You were, whether you want to admit it or not."

"Well yeah." I pulled away from his grasp, immediately hit by the chill of mall air-conditioning. "I miss working, but I couldn't do it anymore. Things were getting too obvious. I was missing every other day at work and shoes weren't doing the trick anymore. Once I hit about five-six, I started getting bad anxiety."

"I remember that," Erik said with a frown. "It killed me inside to see you going through that when I couldn't do anything to help. It's still killing me now."

"Hmmm . . ."

My mind drifted to when things had started becoming noticeable . . .

I REMEMBERED HOW IT FELT when his arms went around my hips as I was getting ready for work.

"Hey, I'm not trying to sound mean or anything, but aren't you supposed to be thicker than this?" Erik had asked, pinching my hip between a finger and thumb.

I remembered swatting at him. "I beg your pardon?" I said sharply, still smiling. I kept staring at the mirror as I finished off my mascara and checked my eyebrow ring. Through the reflection I could see that Erik was trying to figure something out. "I shouldn't look any thinner, it's not like I'm trying to lose weight."

"I assumed that," Erik said before resting his chin on my shoulder from behind me.

At that time I wasn't sure what was happening, but I could definitely see what Erik saw. I looked smaller. Erik was always bigger than me, but since I had moved into his apartment, he seemed bigger than before. I couldn't tell whether it was because I was uncomfortable with him or whatever, but I felt smaller.

"You've been eating, haven't you?"

"Of course I have," I spoke to his reflection in the mirror. "You know me; I can't stop eating." He pulled my body closer to his and breath hit my collarbone.

"I assumed that. Lils, I don't know if this makes sense, but you feel smaller."

He ran a hand under my shirt and his knuckles ran across my rib cage, causing me to shiver. I closed my eyes, not wanting to see my ecstasy in the mirror. I didn't want to admit it but I had been thinking the same thing. My clothes were getting looser and longer and I found myself wearing my old platform shoes that I had sworn never to wear once I hit five foot, ten inches my freshman year of high school.

"I . . . I don't know, babe. Maybe you're getting taller?" I tried to guess.

"I'm not. Look at your clothes." He pulled up my shirt, exposing my skin.

"Hey! Not now! I'm about to go to work!" I squeaked. "I have the Saturday bar shift. I can't show up late."

Erik narrowed his eyes. "I would say I'm not in the mood, but that would be a lie. Besides," he continued. "Look how your pants are sitting."

My once super-tight black skinny jeans hung dangerously low on my hips. I pulled down my Tate Langdon tank to hide the evidence.

"So I'll start wearing belts," I said and reached to the nearest one hanging on the wall. I slid the leather through the loops, setting my pants higher. "Happy now?"

"No, actually, I'm not." His eyebrows pushed together as though it pained him to make his next statement. "You . . . you're shorter."

I tried to wave him off. "That doesn't even make sense. I'm not shorter. I'm fine. You're being crazy." He rested one hand on my collarbone before lowering his head to kiss me on the neck. I shivered.

"I don't think I'm being crazy. I was always taller than you, I know that, but you feel smaller, lately. And your shoes," he said accusingly as he pulled up my pant leg with his Dr. Marten. "Since when do you wear heels?"

I kicked my leg so the hem fell. "They aren't heels. They're wedges."

"Same thing. Why are you wearing them?"

I shrugged. "I just felt like wearing them, I guess."

"I thought you said you didn't want to be any taller."

I tried to walk away and he easily grabbed my shoulder and turned me back to face him. Heat rushed to my face as I realized I had to tilt my chin higher to take him in. Swallowing, I turned away.

"You always talk about how you hate that you're almost six feet tall," Erik continued, reaching to grab my face. "And now you're wearing heels?"

"Wedges."

"Whatever! The point is, it's weird." He stepped back and crossed his arms. "Take them off."

More heat. More embarrassment. "What?"

"Take off your shoes. I want to see something."

"I'm going to work. I need the shift."

"Take. Off. Your. Shoes."

"Is that a command, Mr. Larkin?"

"Maybe it is."

"You're not my dad; I don't have to listen to you."

"Then listen to yourself—let me see you without your shoes. You know you're worried about something, otherwise you wouldn't be wearing them in the first place."

"You're being paranoid."

"I don't care. Take off your shoes."

"Will you let me go to work if I do?" I pulled out my high tech phone and fumbled to find the time on the screen. I missed my flip phone. "I'll tell him I'm stuck in traffic, but that'll only buy me fifteen, twenty minutes tops."

Erik didn't relent. "Shoes. Off. Please."

I rolled my eyes, shifting back and forth on my heels a few times. He wasn't going to let up. He wasn't going to let this go. And as much as I fought him, I'm glad he didn't. I'm glad he pushed because who knows how long I could have denied everything? Sliding off the wedges, I kicked them across the room and stood there glaring at him.

The look on his face in the moment was something I never forgot.

Confusion. Fear. Horror.

He took a deep breath, and drank me in with those intense blue eyes. "W-what . . . what the hell?" he asked. "It's not possible. You're . . ."

I tried to play it off. "I'm shorter. Yes I know."

"Why didn't you say anything?"

"What could I have said?"

"Something!" He raked a long hand through his hair, ruining the style, but he didn't seem to care. "Why didn't you tell me, Lils?"

I shrugged and reached for a necklace. "I guess I was afraid you'd overreact."

"Overreact? You're damn right I'm going to overreact! What the hell?"

He stormed up to my side and grasped my chin in his hand. His touch was never rough, but the strength in his fingers felt more powerful than it had even a few weeks ago.

"You weren't this short when I met you."

"Yes, I'm aware of that, dammit," I said and pulled away from him.

"So . . . what?"

"Erik, I don't know what's happening. You're asking me for answers, when I don't even know the right questions."

"When did it start?"

I shrugged. "Honestly, I can't remember."

"You have to remember something. You knew. You knew this was happening to you." He brandished his hand up and down my frame. "The shoes. You knew."

"It was little things at first, Erik. I didn't think anything about it. Clothes getting looser, shoes sliding off, rings not fitting right." I shrugged. "I guess I just kinda assumed it would stop eventually."

"Well, how do you feel? Mentally, I mean? Emotionally?"

I shrugged. "I feel fine. I'm sure this is nothing." I turned away and started back towards my shoes, but Erik easily wrapped his hand around my entire upper arm.

"You're not going to work."

"I need the shift."

He rolled his eyes. "Not this again, Lils. You don't need the shift. I make more than enough—"

"I don't want to rely on you for money. You're not my husband. And if this . . . if this really is something then I really need to keep making money so I can pay my damn medical bills. I can't call off work every time I have a cough."

His eyes narrowed. "This is a bit more than a cough, Lily."

"We don't know if *this*," I motioned to myself, "is anything."

"I'm calling your boss." In one swift movement, his phone was in-hand.

"No!" I screamed and ran towards him. He easily held the phone above my head which gave me actual pause.

"You can't reach it, can you? You used to be able to."

I lowered my hands to my sides. "I could reach it if I wanted to."

"Liar."

"I'm not lying!"

"Give me your license."

"What for?" I snapped. "I can still drive."

"I want to see the height listed on your license."

Oh. I pulled my *Black Butler* wallet out of my back pocket and handed it to him. His phone chimed.

"You're not going in today."

I rolled my eyes and pretended that I wasn't bothered. "Fine."

Erik scrutinized my license the same way he used to read classics like *Paradise Lost* and *The Iliad.* His lips parted and closed several times and he did the same with his eyes. I wanted to leap inside his brain, desperate to figure out what he was thinking.

"Your license says that you're six-feet even," Erik read.

"I'm not that tall. I'd say five foot, eleven and a half inches."

Erik couldn't stop himself from snorting. "Gotta add the half, eh?"

"Shut up." Nervousness crept up into my voice and I cleared my throat. "So what now? How do we figure out how tall I am now?"

"I've got a tape measure in the bathroom."

I arched my brow. "Measuring something private?" I joked, weakly.

"Always the comedian, my Lily," he said seriously, leaving the room. He was back in a minute. "Stand up against the wall."

"I like when you get bossy." I did as I was told. Carefully, Erik pulled open the tape and measured me from the floor to the top of my head. "What? What does it say?"

"You said five foot, eleven and a half, right?"

"I did."

The tape measure snapped back into the holder. "Lily, according to this you're five foot, seven."

My playful nature fell away. "That's impossible. I'm five foot, eleven."

"Not anymore you're not," Erik said.

"You must be using it wrong."

"It's a tape measure. I think I can use it properly."

"I'm going to work. I started gathering up my things.

"I already called you off. And I'm calling Mark."

"I don't need to see another one of your snooty doctor friends. I'm sure it's nothing but some . . . some weird thing! It'll go away."

"If that's true, then there's no harm in checking into it, is there?"

It may have been a question, but there was a finality in Erik's voice that couldn't have said more of the opposite.

Playtime was over. Sarcasm was wasted. Humor was lost.

I wanted to argue, but four lost inches was something I could no longer ignore. I narrowed my eyes. "Fine. I suppose there's no harm checking into . . . whatever this is. I'm sure it's nothing."

"EARTH TO LILY!" ERIK BELLOWED.

I pulled away from the painful memory and shook my head. "Sorry, I was a million miles away."

"I can tell. What were you thinking about?" he asked.

"Oh, I was thinking about what we were talking about earlier. Having to leave work, not wanting anyone to see me. That stuff."

"I see," Erik said thickly. "Which is why we're here."

"Which is why we're here."

"You still think about why this is happening to you?"

I nodded. "Sometimes, but there's no real point, is there? We know as much now as we did then."

He sighed. "I suppose that's true."

"Erik, I know you said you want to pretend that things are

okay, but I can't walk around like nothing's happening. Like Fire Engine lady didn't think I was a kid."

"Fire Engine lady? You mean Dallas?"

I rolled my eyes. "You saw how she treated me. She thought I was a kid."

"She doesn't know you."

"What does it matter if they know me or not? What do you think Gabe would think if he knew what was happening? Or Ava? How would they act?"

"Supportive?" Erik guessed.

"What a charming thought." I grimaced at the idea of Ava treating me like one of those kids who came into American Wake. How she hovered over them and all but pinched their cheeks. How every statement sounded like a question because of how squeaky her voice sounded when she tried to coo at them.

"They'd probably be more supportive than you think."

"I don't want to talk about it anymore," I snapped, forcibly pushing away thoughts of Ava settling me in a booster seat. "It's done now."

"If you would give people a chance—"

"I don't want to shop for clothes where people could recognize me," I interrupted. "I'm sorry. This is the way it needs to be."

"Yes, I know this what you want. I also think you need to see the good in people, trust people. You don't have to go through this alone."

"I'm not alone."

"You know what I mean, Lils."

I grabbed his hand. "Erik, what's happening to me isn't normal. You know that it's not. I can't really trust anyone. Except you."

"And Mark."

"And your family," I added, not wanting to express my slight distrust in Mark.

"You know people still ask about you at American Wake," Erik said, lowering his voice.

"They want to know where I'm at." It was a fact, not a question.

"Wouldn't you be curious if someone suddenly disappeared off the face of the earth? Lily, people know we got married."

"And you tell them I'm a private person like we agreed on. Don't you?"

"I do, but I'm worried that it's not enough. It doesn't make sense for a man to marry a woman and then hide her from the world."

"It makes perfect sense. I got the guy and now I want to stay in the house like a good housewife. I'm sure more women do it than you think."

"I hate hiding you."

"And I hate hiding," I agreed. "It still has to be done."

He nodded slowly. "Doesn't change my answer. I don't want to make you do anything that would make you feel uncomfortable, but it doesn't make it any less hard."

"You can't even imagine how hard this is for me, babe."

He gently squeezed my hand. "I know. I just want to be a good husband to you. I didn't marry you for the hell of it. I married you because I love you. I want to be there for you."

"I know. But you know what would be really great?" His facial expression made it obvious that he knew what I wanted and I couldn't help chuckling.

"Oh, what now? You're hungry, aren't you?"

I burst out laughing. "It's dinner time! Aren't people supposed to eat?"

"You want to get it to-go, or do you want to eat here?"

I grinned. "I'm still pretty tall, I don't mind eating here."

He bent down and pressed his lips against mine. That feeling never got old. This man—this tall, perfect and regal man wanted to kiss me. He wanted to marry me. He wanted to be there for me. Fate sure was a cruel bitch if this was all meant to be nothing more than a story I could look back on fondly in a few years.

"I'm glad to hear that. It's going to be terrible when we have to stop going out."

"*If,* Erik," I said quickly, surprised that I wasn't the one drawing to the worst conclusion. "*If* I have to stop going out."

"Right. If."

We made our way to the food court in silence with his statement still bothering me.

If Erik was already becoming used to the idea that I was shrinking, I wondered how far he imagined this going. Until I was the size of a child? There's a two-foot tall woman living in India, surely it would not come to that. I tried to imagine becoming any smaller than this. It was terrifying. I couldn't stand being so much shorter than my husband, and I hated the looks we got when I couldn't shake them off with a muttered curse. We were already so different, and now our height difference gave gawkers one more reason to feel okay about staring openly at us.

The stares hurt. I was scared, and there wasn't anything I could do about it.

"If," I repeated to myself as he led me to the escalator, standing two steps below me.

"It will stop, Lils. It has to stop at some point. Mark's doing everything he can. There has to be some sort of medical explanation for this."

I tried to nod with a brave face, leaning forward to kiss his cheek. "Yeah, I mean I can't keep shrinking until I'm the size of a damn child, can I? I'm already close enough."

"You're not that small."

"I may be soon, if this doesn't stop."

"It'll stop."

"Yeah," I said as Erik turned around to decide between chicken teriyaki or beef burrito.

I wanted to reach out and run my fingers through his dark hair, pull him close to me and make him promise on his life that this couldn't go on forever. Helplessly, I watched my husband coast down the escalator a few steps ahead of me.

He may as well been riding alone.

No one would think that he was mine.

Three

50 Inches / 4 Feet, 2 Inches

"I WANT TO go home," I mumbled as we sat down. "Erik, people are staring."

"They aren't staring at you. They're staring at both of us," Erik said.

"I shouldn't have let you talk me into getting dinner. People probably think I'm your kid."

Erik shook his head. "I don't think so. You're still perfectly proportioned."

I snorted. "Stop trying to be so reasonable."

"It's true, though."

"I'm only as perfectly proportioned as someone barely four feet tall can be."

"You're still amazing to me," Erik said in a low voice, lifting his water glass up to his lips. "Let's see how this goes, okay?"

I squirmed in the seat across from Erik. What was I thinking when I agreed to go out to dinner with him? It was late enough and I admitted that I wanted some greasy scrambled eggs and pancakes, but I didn't think so many people would gawk.

At four foot two inches I shouldn't have been surprised. I couldn't *really* pass for a woman anymore, and because of my proportions I didn't look much like a child, either. People who walked past our table at The Greasy Spoon knitted their brows together and whispered amongst themselves.

Our waitress must have been younger than me and she eyed up Erik like he was available on the menu with a hot cup of coffee or an icy milkshake. The way she hungrily licked her lips, she must have wanted to jump him right then and there in the booth.

"What can I get you, sweetie?" she purred, locking her brown eyes on his.

Erik's one eyebrow arched upward before he fixed me with a desperate look. "I think she wants some breakfast. Don't you?"

I coolly nodded towards the waitress. Her amiable expression slipped as she took me in.

"We do have a breakfast special for late nights," she said, sounding slightly miffed. "Say, you mind if I ask you a question?"

"I rather you didn't," I grumbled before smiling fakely. "Sure, what is it?"

"How old are you?"

I sucked in my breath, annoyed to be asked a question so openly. Seriously, Chocolate Eye Bitch was already on my last nerve and I didn't even have my cranberry juice yet.

"Uh, she'll have the egg special with pancakes," Erik said quickly. "And I'll have the sirloin with a salad."

Chocolate Eye Bitch turned back to Erik. "You know, it's always nice to see people taking out their . . . niece?" She guessed, smirking. "Actually, that doesn't make a lot of sense. I mean, unless you're adopted? Or an in-law?"

"I'm his wife," I growled, handing over my menu. *Bitch.*

She giggled and placed a hand on her hip. Acrylic nails. "And it's so cute that you think that. One day you'll have to realize that you can't marry—"

"It's true," Erik interrupted. "She's my wife. She's the same age as me."

Chocolate Eyes broke out into a huge smile. "Are you serious? But you're—"

"I'm short, but I'm not a kid," I said sharply. "In fact, I'm probably older than you."

"Lils, stop. It's not worth it." He turned to the Chocolate Eyes as she put a fake nail up to her fake looking lips. "Could you please . . . ?" Erik trailed off; making it as obvious as he could that he wanted her to leave without breaking that professional demeanor he liked to sport in public.

"The cooks are gonna throw a fit," Chocolate Eyes said under her breath. She waved those wild fake nails around and I worried one was going to fly off and blind me. "No, I'm sorry, I'm sorry. I'll get your order ready. Egg special with pancakes and a sirloin with salad." She quickly jotted it down. "Dressing?"

"French."

"Sure thing, Kitten."

"Wait!" I couldn't resist calling out to her. She turned around and peered down. "What do you mean the cooks are going to have a fit?"

"Oh, you heard that?" She flushed. "Sorry, Kitten."

"What did you mean by it?" I snapped over her.

"Since you got here," she began to explain before jutting a thumb over her shoulder, "they've been placing bets."

"Bets?" Erik repeated.

"How old your, um . . . wife is. Some of them thought she was older than she looked. Some of us kind of thought she was a kid, but her face doesn't look that young." She giggled behind her hand which further infuriated me.

I wondered if anyone had bet on me standing up on the cheap, plastic booth and punching her in the nose.

Erik must have felt my anger because he reached over the table and gently took my hand in his. I jerked my head around to glare at him and his face immediately calmed me down. Chocolate Eyes Bitch and The Greasy Spoon . . . they weren't worth making a scene.

I was a freak, after all.

Somewhat defeated by that painful conclusion, I settled down and sheepishly mouthed an apology.

Nodding as soon as he knew he had calmed me down, he couldn't resist doing the 'man' thing and defending me. It was a good and bad thing. Personally, I wanted to pop this bitch, but I also wanted to kiss my husband for doing my dirty work.

"Please don't talk about my wife like that," he said firmly.

The waitress flushed as he spoke to her. "Y-yes, I'm sorry. I'll get your food ready. You know what?" She smiled nervously, obviously trying to save her tip. "I'll get you each a milkshake. It'll be on the house because of my rudeness. What would you like?"

"Vanilla," I muttered.

"Chocolate," Erik said, sharing a secret grin with me.

Erik always picked chocolate and I always chose vanilla.

The waitress didn't get it.

"Coming right up," she said. "I'll be back."

Despite witnessing Erik go into uber sexy 'protective' mode, when our milkshakes and food arrived, I was hardly in the mood to eat. Everyone who passed the window, every person, or family walking into the diner seemed to do a double take. It was possible that no one was looking, but that's what it felt like. Eyes burned into my back. Disapproving glances shot into my chest. And confused conversations made my ears bleed.

I couldn't tell what was real and what was false.

It all hurt.

"I want to go now, Erik," I pleaded, hoping that my hands

wouldn't shake. A panic attack knocked on my door. I tried to hide behind the metaphorical couch. "Can't you see how uncomfortable I am?"

He lowered his fork. "They're probably only trying to figure out how old you are." He shot me a wolfish grin. "Maybe you should roll up your sleeves and let them decide."

I tried not to smile as just a few sentence from his lips seemed to calm the voices and stares. That grin relaxed my nerves in ways that he would never understand. Erik Larkin was better than any dose of Klonopin.

"That's not funny, moron. If anything that will make them look more."

He laughed. "I say go for it. What's the worst that could happen?"

I enjoyed a small chuckle with him before dusting off my hands. "My husband the comedian. Pause your act for a minute; I have to go to the bathroom. I'll be right back."

His eyebrow arched. "You want me to come with you?" His jovial mood suddenly vanished.

"It's the bathroom," I grumbled and began to pull myself out of the booth. I swear I heard people shifting to get a better look. *Not real. It wasn't real. No one could be that interested.* "Dammit. What am I, some sort of sideshow with dinner?"

"People can't help being curious," Erik offered off-handedly, glaring at several gawkers.

Once my newer, smaller and genuine Converse hit the ground, I glanced up at Erik in the raised booth. "I'll be right back."

"Be careful—er, I mean, I'll see you in a bit."

"Carol!" A woman called out.

I started to turn and my world rocked violently.

Suddenly, the main floor of The Greasy Spoon was fuzzy and at the wrong angle. I shook my head and things began to refocus.

I was on the ground.

"Ouch," I muttered, finding a large child with fat cheeks standing over me.

"I'm sorry, I'm sorry, sir!"

A woman came up from behind and scooped up the gawking child in her arms. The girl wasn't as tall as me, but broader of shoulder and heavier. And probably still in kindergarten.

She had easily knocked me over and I could feel a small bump forming on my temple where the side of my face hit the concrete floor. I stared up at the woman who was looking over my head at Erik.

"She gets so hyper over the littlest things. Are you alright, dear?" she asked kindly, peering down at me. She offered her hand, but I instinctively crawled away from her.

I nearly squeaked when a pair of large hands seized me gently around the waist, and easily set me standing me upright. The woman crouched down to my level, still holding the child in her arms.

"Oh my goodness. Her forehead," she said to Erik. "I'm so sorry, is there anything I can do?"

I rubbed my head, feeling like a child, watching adults talk over them. Erik's hands gripped my shoulders.

"You could start by apologizing not to me, but rather to my wife," he said.

"Your *wife?*" The woman exclaimed and peered at me closely. I turned my face away from her and turned to Erik.

"I want to go home . . . *now*," I begged. Tears threatened to spring from my eyes. I blinked hard. I couldn't take any more.

"Alright, alright," Erik finally agreed and began fumbling with his wallet.

"No, no," the woman said before handing him two twenty-dollar bills. "I'll take care of this. It's the least I can do. I'm sorry. I'm so sorry . . . ma'am," she stammered before she couldn't help herself and looked back to Erik. "If it's anything serious, please don't hesitate to contact me." She handed a card to him. "I feel terrible. I thought she was a child. So did Carol, I'm sure. I'm sure she only wanted to play."

"Erik," I grumbled, pulling my large coat off of the booth. "I'm ready."

As he shifted to put on his coat, I was surrounded by both him and the stammering woman with the chubby cheeked daughter. Erik hovered over me, as did the woman and the child in her arms. I felt a horrible desire to stand behind Erik and peek out to look at the woman and her daughter, but such a thing certainly wouldn't help negate my child-like appearance.

I couldn't help it, though.

I needed him.

I felt safe with him and I wanted to get home and go to the bathroom and put some ice on the lump forming on my head.

"Right," Erik said softly. "You need anything else? You want them to box up the leftovers?"

"No. Let's go." I stalked towards the door before anything else could happen.

I shouldn't have gone out. This world was simply too dangerous for me. A child had nearly given me a concussion and adult spoke over me like I wasn't even there. I couldn't handle it anymore.

This world . . . it wasn't made for someone like me.

The walk across the parking lot was silent, and when Erik reached down to take my hand, I jerked out of his grasp.

"Don't even bother, you don't want to hurt your back," I snapped as I stood in front of the car, waiting for him to unlock it.

"Are you okay? Do you want me to take you to the hospital?" he asked carefully as he opened the door. "Do you think you have a concussion?"

I shook my head. "I think I'm okay. I was surprised as hell; I never realized how big kids were. I didn't even think about how rowdy they could be."

We settled into our respective seats.

"Well, it's a good thing that we don't have any, right?" he asked lightly.

"We don't, but it doesn't mean that you won't later." Erik's large hand froze close the key ignition.

"What's that supposed to mean?"

"Nothing. I have to go to the bathroom and my freaking head is bleeding. Can we go home without the fourth degree?"

He started the car, and glanced over as we stopped at one of the various stop signs. "Are you sure you're okay?"

I nodded.

"And that comment you made about kids—"

"Don't be ridiculous. I can't give you children now," I said curtly.

"Well yeah, I realize that, but you mumbled something about me having kids later?"

I stiffened. Just thinking about what I had to say next hurt more than I thought. "With someone else."

"There won't be anyone else."

I blew a loud sigh through my lips. "I want to stop talking about it."

Erik pulled into the driveway.

"There is one thing that I want to talk to you about," I said.

"I thought you had to use the bathroom. I also have to check on your head," he said. "Maybe Mark should come over and take another—"

"Stop, Erik. Please. I don't want to see anyone else. I just want to tell you something and I really need you to listen." I gripped my hands into fists as the atmosphere in the car grew heavy.

"What is it?" Erik asked. I could barely see his face in the dark.

"I can't go out anymore. It's getting too hard for me." Erik leaned over into the passenger seat to catch my words. "Please."

For some reason I expected him to argue. To crack a joke about how this would all stop and that I was looking too much into things. He stared straight ahead.

His shoulders slumped. "Okay. I kind of figured you would bring this up eventually. Every time we go out, I worry it's the last time unless this shrinking thing lets up."

Shrinking thing. Ugh, it was a thing now. I didn't know what hurt more. That it was a thing, or that it had to be acknowledged in the first place.

"Well, it hasn't. We can't pretend anymore. I can't pretend anymore. I'm shrinking, and I'm not safe around people. Getting hit by that girl felt liked getting run over by an orc—I could have fractured my skull."

This pulled his attention away from the apartment straight ahead. "You're right."

He reached towards my temple and his fingertips brushed the area around the wound. My breath caught as his tired ice blue eyes sought out my hazel ones in the shadows. I took in and released a trembling breath as he continued to brush his fingers against my face.

"I'm relieved it wasn't worse."

Something between a laugh and a sob rose in my chest as I lifted my eyes to meet his. "Can you understand though? I can't do these things with you. I can't go out for coffee, I can't go to the bookstores, I can't . . . I can't do those things anymore."

He nodded and traced his finger up and down my cheek. "I know. It's not like I want you to get hurt either. And I see what you mean."

"Good."

Come here," he said suddenly.

"Excuse me?"

He motioned for me to come closer to him. "Give me a hug," he said with a tentative grin. "I'm sorry for what happened earlier.

You will still hug me, won't you?"

I unsnapped my seat belt. "Of course I'll still hug you," I laughed and settled into his lap. It was strange to see his long legs tucked underneath the steering wheel while his huge hand gently ran through my dreadlocks. There was already so much of him, but I enjoyed being held like this, four feet tall or not. He was my husband, after all.

But reality had to come in and remind me not to enjoy anything too much.

"Erik . . ." I said seriously.

"Hmmm?"

"Please don't make go anywhere unless we absolutely have to."

He kissed the top of my head. "Nowhere else, Lils. I couldn't deny you anything. I'll let my parents know."

I pulled away with wide eyes. "Your parents? Why do they need to know anything?"

He smiled and kissed me again. "I need to start making arrangements."

"Arrangements for what?" He shushed me, pulling me closer to him. "Erik," I said to his soft black sweater.

"Yes, Lils?"

I was about to argue with him, but I was simply too tired. "I still have to go to the bathroom," was all I could say.

His chuckle shook my entire body.

Four

42 Inches / 3 feet, 6 Inches

"SAD MOVIES AGAIN, eh?" Erik asked as he came through the front door to find me on the couch.

"They're not sad," I said, waving my hand at the screen. "They're beautiful. I still can't get over the things that couples go through to stay together. It's so touching."

"*Touching?*" He repeated with a smirk before glaring at the television. "Damn you!" He shouted dramatically to the screen. "What have you been doing to my wife?"

I couldn't help laughing. "Shut up," I said, smiling. "There's nothing wrong with romantic movies. They're lovely."

Erik rolled his eyes, remaining playful. "Lovely, she says. You have been watching too many of these movies."

"Oh, leave me be," I muttered, dabbing my eyes with a tissue.

Erik hung up his coat and plunked down next to me, causing my body to bounce in the seat. He turned sheepish as I collected myself.

"Sorry about that."

"It's fine. So how was work?" I asked, pausing the movie.

I had taken to watching sad and overly romantic movies since Erik had agreed not to force me to go anywhere with him. He had signed me up for a program through our cable company so I could rent as many movies as I wanted off the TV. I never saw so many love stories before in my life! I wasn't really allowed to watch much TV growing up, and there was something comforting about crying over something other than my condition. Over the past few weeks I watched couples overcome race, age, religion, sexual orientation, social status, and more. Their soppy stories gave me hope that Erik and I could actually have a shot.

"Work was work," he said, unbuttoning the top two buttons on his shirt and revealing what still looked like an amazing body.

I bit my lip and tried to focus.

"What about you? What'd you do all day?" He paused with for a false dramatic effect. "Other than watch love stories?"

I shifted awkwardly on the couch. "Hey, it's hard to do other things."

He glanced towards the laptop he had left next to me on the couch "Did you try going on the computer?"

"No."

"Did you order lunch from any of the places I set tabs up at? Nino's has a mean pizza—"

"No, I wasn't that hungry—"

"Liar."

"I'm serious. I wasn't hungry."

His dark eyebrow was arched. "I doubt that."

I shrugged. "Plus, I guess I just didn't want anyone to see me."

"Did you—"

"Alright, I'm guilty!" I proclaimed in an overly-dramatic voice. "I sat around and watched sappy movies all day. Are you happy?

I admit it! It turns out I'm a sucker for sappy movies and I never realized it." I huffily crossed my arms, but peeking at Erik out of the corner of my eye, he was smiling. "Damn you," I laughed. "I can't help it. I never had a chance to watch these types of movies before. Or much of any movies."

The shine in his eyes dulled slightly whenever I mentioned my past. "That's right. You didn't see a lot of movies growing up, did you?"

I shrugged it off. "It was never a big priority when I was in foster care. And once I was able to work, I worked like crazy. I didn't have time to find out if Robert Redford was going to suck it up and stick with Barbara Streisand."

His eyes softened. "He doesn't."

"I know that now."

He hummed. "Sorry, Lils. Sometimes I forget that you and I had very different upbringings."

"Is that even possible? One would think that it would be impossible to forget—"

"I do sometimes, and I hate that I forget—"

I waved my hands around. "I know. It's fine. All I'm saying is that it's kind of nice to watch something . . . or anything for that matter and not have to worry about wasting time or energy."

Erik chuckled, but there was something uncomfortable about his laugh. "I'm glad you don't have to worry about that kind of stuff. You shouldn't have to. I guess you leaving work wasn't such a terrible idea, huh?"

"Work wasn't the same after you left anyway," I said, snuggling up to him. "That day sucked."

"It couldn't have sucked that bad. Lukas ordered that cake and if I recall, there was someone who really liked his choice of red velvet and cream cheese frosting. There was a certain *someone* who ate at least five or six pieces."

"I did not eat six pieces of cake!" I yelped, punching his

shoulder. "I ate a few, yes."

"A few can mean six."

"And a few can mean two! I like cake!"

He laughed. "Cake aside, are you sure you don't miss any of the girls? I mean, it's not like you couldn't call or text them if you wanted to. Ava would probably be happy to hear from you."

"She'll be fine."

"She could pass the word and let everyone know how you're doing. It will give you a chance to talk to someone else during the day so you're not here all alone, watching sad movies."

"I'm sure most of them haven't given my absence a second thought. People come and go from American Wake all the time." I turned. "I mean who have you honestly talked to since you left there? Did *you* text or call anyone lately?"

"Well, no," he laughed uneasily. "I'll admit it, I didn't. Once I got my 'real' job, I kind of forgot about that place." Noticing the frown on my face he went on. "But that wasn't a temporary job for you, Lils and whether you want to admit it or not, you liked your title. I was nothing more than a clumsy waiter."

"You did have your moments, didn't you?" I snickered fondly, remembering a particularly funny moment when he tripped over his own shoe and landed dangerously close to the pudding at the salad bar.

"Only when you were watching." He paused for a moment then stood up suddenly. "So how about this? I'm going to change, put on something more comfortable and then . . . I want to watch the mushiest, *gushiest* movie you've seen so far. I'm talking total sob fest. Make me cry, baby."

"I don't cry during World War II movies like you," I chuckled.

"That was *one* movie, Lils," Erik said, smiling. "It caught me off guard. Seriously though, I want to see something that you think will have me reaching for the tissues."

I covered my mouth with my hand to hide a snorting laugh.

"You're not kidding, are you?"

"Erik Larkin does not kid. I am deathly serious and scary and stuff," he said, doing his best to not to laugh. "I want to see what you've been up to."

I rolled my eyes. "Oh, I've been up to a lot of things. There was the Clark Gable time, and then the emo vampires and then . . ." As I snuck over a glance at Erik, his expression wasn't exactly promising. "Okay, okay," I laughed and began to scroll with the remote trying to find the perfect movie.

"If you pick emo vampires, I'll be crying before the movie even starts."

"Consider them off the table."

Erik gently touched the small of my back for a moment from behind on the couch. "Give me a few minutes, okay?"

A chill danced up my spine and I tried to remain focused. "Sure."

Once he was gone I gathered my thoughts.

Since turning fifteen, I worked full time. I had worked at fast-food joints, retail places pimping out character tees, outdoors trimming Christmas trees, and indoors shelling out cookies for four bucks a piece. It was odd, but not altogether unpleasant to not have to work anymore. I woke up when I wanted, put on something I wanted to watch and if it was boring, I fell asleep. If it was good, I paid close attention and waited for Erik to come home and spend time with me. I could have made dinner if he wanted it—it was certainly not impossible—but he insisted on picking things up or cooking himself.

I never had a life like this before, and even though it was hor-rible to still be shrinking, it was a pleasant distraction to take on the role of a Larkin housewife. He only wanted me to be happy. It was still hard on the nights that he went out with friends, but those nights were becoming rarer and rarer. It was hard watching him leave for work every morning, and some days I would go a little stir crazy without any human interaction.

I wished that Erik could have been around more. That was my one complaint.

Other than the fact that I was barely three and half feet tall, of course.

"You ready?" Erik asked when he walked into the room wearing a thin white t-shirt and mesh basketball shorts straight out of the 1990s. "Did you pick out something that'll make me cry? I'm up for the challenge!" He reached over and set a tissue box in front of him before flopping heavily on the couch.

"You look nice," I couldn't help blurting out.

His quizzical expression danced between me and his attire. "You feelin' alright, Lils? I'm wearing some crap to relax in. I can't possibly look nice." He smirked. "If you want to see something nice, I'll go put on a pair of your skinny jeans—"

"It's just nice to see you, I guess," I said, sliding next to him.

He wrapped a long arm around my shoulders and pulled me towards him. The scent of citrus and grass hit my nostrils, which was odd since he had worked all day and didn't always smell the freshest after a long day working for the man.

"It does get kind of hard not having you around."

"Really?" he asked above my head. "I thought you were digging the whole 'stay at home and watch movies' deal. I didn't think that you'd want to see me more."

I hugged him as best I could. "It's not like I see anyone else."

"My parents would love to see you—"

"I can't stand the idea of your mom or dad seeing me like this," I interrupted. "I was trying to say that I miss you. It's different when I was working, I suppose."

"So, you want to see me more? Is that what you're saying?"

I nodded.

"You wanna try saying that to me?" he asked, tilted my head up with a single finger. "You're hinting at it, but I'd love to hear you actually say the words."

"Come on, ass. I want to watch soppy movies, not live in one."
I tried to pull my face away from his touch, and he remained firm.

"All I want is for you to say it to me, Lils. You have no idea how
much it would mean to hear those words."

The vulnerability in his eyes was straight out of a 1950s classic
Hollywood film. Hell, my husband was straight out of 50s classic
movie.

Who was I to resist?

"Erik . . . I . . . I really want to see you more."

His expression was a reminder as to how much I hated the
way he made me feel. So damn cheesy.

But more importantly, it was a reminder of how much I loved
it.

Five

38 Inches / 3 Feet, 2 Inches

"I CAN'T THANK you guys enough for letting me do this."

The woman's voice that answered was faint, but still distinguishable. "It's the least we can do. The poor girl. Has anything like this ever happened before?"

"Mark's been looking into it, and I have to say that it doesn't look good. It's been eight months and she hasn't slowed down. I keep hoping I'll wake up the next day and she'll be the same height as the day before, but no. Even if it's only a millimeter, she's still shrinking."

"How tall is she now?" a new and slightly older voice asked, sounding like a more mature version of Erik.

"About three feet."

"My God," the older man answered. "How are *you* handling it?"

My pulse quickened as I waited for Erik's response. My

husband grabbed the back of his neck and rubbed the area, before absently tugging on his jet black hair. I knew he wanted to say something, but he was probably worried about me hearing his response. He probably thought I was asleep, and he had every reason to be cautious. I stood near the doorway of his office as he sat and spoke to his parents through Skype. Erik's mom and dad were nice enough to help us financially so that Erik could be around a lot more, but my change in height had become so serious that they had decided to rent us a home out in the sticks so we wouldn't be bothered.

Or rather so *I* wouldn't be bothered.

I refused to let anyone but Erik see me now. Few people knew about my condition and it wasn't like I had a family I could go to. Erik's parents wanted to come by and talk to me, but I was too ashamed. It felt like I had done something wrong and was being punished. I hated watching the world shoot up around me in all directions.

I chewed on my lower lip, making sure to hang back so Erik wouldn't catch me eavesdropping while I so desperately wanted to hear his answer. I tugged on the heavy ring that now hung around my neck on a delicate chain.

"It's hard," he said finally, lowering his head. "This shouldn't be happening to her. I don't know how much longer I can watch."

I gasped as his words pierced like a dull blade or shot of cheap vodka. It was only a matter of time before he left me. I poked my head through the doorway and Erik's mother tilted her head on the computer screen.

"Lily?" she called out and Erik shot around in his seat.

I jumped as his light blue eyes settled on my frightened frame and guilty expression. It was a small movement, but everything was magnified now. He looked caught and I didn't know whether to be more upset with him, or more upset with myself for spying.

"Lils!" he blurted. "It's not what you think—it's not what it sounds like."

"Yes it is," I said as I became more and more saddened at the idea of not having him. "You don't think you can do this anymore."

"I didn't say that, what I meant was—"

"Forget it. I don't blame you for saying it."

"Lils, you don't understand. Let me explain—"

"No."

I stepped away from the door frame and took off towards our bedroom. Erik muttered something to his parents and the all-too-familiar sound of a Skype call ending filled my ears, but I still didn't want to talk to him.

I also didn't want to be caught by my husband who was now more than twice my size. I sprinted to the bedroom and pushed the door shut like an angry child.

"Lily," Erik called as his footsteps echoed down the hall.

His steps reminded me of bad foster homes; my pulse quickened as they reverberated through the floor. Cold sweat formed on my forehead and my hands started to tremble.

As the door creaked open I slid under the bed and lay on my stomach, feeling ashamed for acting this way and even more ashamed that I was acting my size.

Like a child.

Erik treaded in softly as I settled down under the center of the bed.

"Lils?" he asked as I huddled under the center of the bed. His feet shifted around the room. "Lils, where are you?"

Tear of humiliation and embarrassment came to my eyes as he walked over to the closet and peered inside. I might have hid there when I was taller, but now I was small enough to fit easily under the bed. Maybe he would think that I had shrunk to nothingness and he could be free of this burden at last. I sniffed audibly and Erik's feet shifted away from the closet and towards the bed.

Caught. I wasn't good at hiding then so I guess it made sense that I wasn't too good at hiding now.

The floor creaked as he padded over and his knees struck the hardwood floor. Carefully, he lowered his face down and his eyes fell on me. He looked hurt and confused, which I didn't quite understand. Wasn't he ashamed of me? Wasn't he ashamed for being in this situation?

"What are you doing down there?" His voice was down to a whisper.

"Waiting," I answered with a frown.

His eyebrow arched. "Waiting for what?"

"Waiting until I shrink down to nothing. That way you don't have to watch this anymore. You won't have to babysit me."

Pain flickered across his face, and his eyes remained locked on mine with a gentleness that nearly broke my heart. I wanted to be held in his arms despite how much they frightened me with their power and strength. I didn't want to be alone, but I couldn't forget what I heard him say a few minutes earlier.

"Lils," he went on, "I think you misunderstood me."

I violently shook my head as he attempted to reach under the bed. I quickly pulled away, and his hand froze in the air for a moment before he pulled it away. I must have recoiled from it like fire. I swallowed.

"I heard what you said, Erik. You said you couldn't watch this anymore. I know what that means. I get that I'm shrinking, but that doesn't mean my brain is. I heard you. I know what you meant."

Erik's eyes lowered to the floor and for a few moments the room was silent. Nothing but the gentle breeze of his breathing. It frightened me just how loud a single breath could sound in my ears.

"What I meant was I hate having to watch this happen to you.

I feel so helpless."

I lifted my head and his cheek was still pressed to the floor. "*You* feel helpless?" I retorted, feeling myself already beginning to cave.

He nodded. "How can I not? I hate that the most important person in my life is going through something so unbelievably awful. I can't bear to watch you shrink every day." He pressed his lips together before he spoke. "I almost wish I could shrink with you."

"Almost?" I smiled sadly. *Even he couldn't commit himself to such a fate.*

"That way we could at least deal with this together. You must feel so alone."

"I am alone," I said, steeling my jaw and not wanting to cry. "There's no one else out there going through this. I don't feel alone, Erik. I *am* alone."

"I know," he muttered, dropping his attention to the knots in the floor for a second time. "Hiding under our bed isn't the solution. Will you please come out from there?"

"What's the point?"

"Lily," he whispered and moved his arm under the bed to touch me. I allowed him to pull me out like a child. He stayed in a crouched position and held me close. I wrapped my arms around his neck and sniffed hard, enjoying the warmth of his body, and the steady thrum of his heart.

"I feel like I'm taking so much away from you," I confessed and I felt him pull me tighter against his chest. My ribs creaked alarmingly, and I tried not to show it. How long before he would have to be concerned about such things? How many months? Or weeks? I buried my face into his shirt and mumbled, "I'm ruining your life."

"Don't start that emo stuff. You're the only thing that makes this life worth living," he said simply, kissing the top of my head. I nuzzled into him.

"You really mean that, don't you?"

"I am weird, aren't I?"

He was trying to lighten the mood, and just because I was so desperate for the air not to get heavy, I relaxed in his grasp. "Just a little, babe. Ugh, and I'm sorry I misunderstood you earlier."

"You have nothing to apologize about, Lils. Love means never having to say you're sorry." He chuckled above my head. "Damn, now you've got me quoting romance movies."

I smiled. "Ali McGraw would be pleased."

"Damn right."

"I am still sorry. I'm so insecure right now. I'm . . . I'm waiting for you to leave me."

"*Leave you?*" Erik asked sharply, losing all the playfulness in his voice. He pulled me out of his embrace and stood me up in front of his face. Cupping my face in his hands, he smoothed away my tears with his thumbs. "Don't be dumb. I'd give up everything for you. My job. My home. My friends. Hell, even my family if they weren't so damn in love with you now. I'm quoting *Love Story* quotes to you with a serious look on my face! Does that sound like a man who's going to leave you?"

I nodded. "A time might come—"

"No, Lils. Marriage is not some temporary deal to me. I'm not going to leave you."

"Until I'm too small to see. Then you may not even realize you're doing it."

"That's not poss . . ." he trailed off. "I h-hope it never comes to that." He kissed the side of my face. "But . . ."

"What?" I was beginning to feel a little better, but Erik's face contorted despite his incredible ability to leap from humor to serious declarations. "What is it?"

"Well . . ." He started rubbing the back of his neck, glimpsing everything in our room except me. "When I was finished talking with my parents, I was going to wake you up so I could ask you something."

My eyebrows knitted together. "Ask me something?"

"More like I wanted to try something, and I'm not sure how you'll feel about it."

"What is it?" I asked nervously. I hesitantly reached out to touch his face. His chin easily filled up my entire hand.

"You're starting to get seriously small now . . ."

My hazel eyes narrowed. "Yes, I know that. Get to the point, Erik."

"I want to pick you up," he blurted, trying to gauge my reaction.

My heart dropped to my bare feet. "You want to what? Are you serious?" I asked hollowly.

"You're not getting any bigger." Heat rushed to his pale cheeks as his eyes flickered up and down my frame. "It might make things easier."

"I'm not a kid," I mumbled.

His eyes met mine. "You know I don't see it that way."

I knew that, but the implication, the reality of it still hurt. "I know you don't, but if we try this, then it means that this really is happening. I'm losing my humanity. I'm becoming a doll."

"No!" Erik grabbed my shoulders and shook his head. "No, that's not it. That's not at all how I see it, Lils."

"Then what is it?"

"I want to feel like I can do something to help. Anything." He paused and I opened my mouth to ask him a question, and he beat me to it. "Aren't you comfortable with me?"

My eyes drifted to the bureau. None of my belongings were on it. Just Erik's. Most of my stuff had been moved into lower level drawers. We were still together, but our things were already a world apart.

"I was," I whispered. "I mean I am! But it's still hard for me. Don't you see how this would be hard for me?"

Erik's expression didn't change. "What changed? Do you see me as a monster already?"

"A monster?" I choked out. "Of course not!"

"There's more to a monster than green skin and yellow eyes," Erik muttered.

"You could never look like a monster to me," I stammered, horrified at the idea of seeing my husband as anything than that. "You're . . . you're everything to me. I'd be lost without you."

"Then let me try, Lils. I know you must be worried that I'll hurt you or something—"

"I know you won't hurt me!" I snapped. "It's weird for me, okay? Being picked up, being carried around." I glanced away. "Even by you." I took in the hands resting on his jeans. They were my husband's hands sure, but they didn't look like the same hands from my memories. They were bigger. Stronger. More danger- ous. It wouldn't be hard for him to accidently hurt me, a fear that seemed more justified every time my tender ribs twinged.

"What's going to happen if you get much smaller?" he chal- lenged, oblivious to my inner turmoil. "Don't you think it will be become even more daunting later?"

My shoulders slumped. He couldn't understand.

I would have to get used to the whole child experience: look- ing like a child, feeling like a child, and being treated like a child by my husband. It was terrible to think that even though we were the same in some ways, we couldn't be more different in others.

I licked my lips before I spoke. "I suppose so."

"Then . . ."

I sighed loudly and met his gaze. Erik Larkin was my husband. I loved him, I needed him, and I wanted to be held by him—even if it meant him holding me in his arms like a child. I stepped clos- er to his seated body and averted my face.

"Okay, but you better be careful."

He lifted his free hand and traced a gentle finger down the

side of my face. His hand tickled slightly.

"Don't tell me you're just as scared as I am?" I tried to tease.

"Scared to pick up my own wife?" he responded, playing along for a moment. Then his face grew serious. "Hell yeah I'm nervous, Lils." He kept his hand tucked under my chin, not allowing me to avoid his gaze. "I don't ever want to hurt you."

"I think we'll be alright. I'm not that small yet."

He nodded. "Okay then," he said softly and, with little ceremony, wrapped his hands around my waist and hips on both sides.

It was such a strange feeling that I gasped. The minute the small sound left my lips, he immediately panicked and his fingers loosened their grip.

"What?" The alarm written all over his face. "Did I do something wrong?"

"No!" I said, fighting a strange desire to giggle. "It feels weird." I reached out and rested my hands on his.

"Isn't weird a bad thing?" he asked in a slightly worried tone.

I loved the look in his ice blue eyes as he gazed at me like I was a porcelain doll. I wasn't used to this type of attention. When I was . . . normal, most men looked at me like I'd either bite their heads off or get all McStabby on them. It wasn't like I tried to be scary, but being almost six feet tall, dark-skinned and sporting dreads, tattoos and piercings, no matter how nice I tried to look, people tended to form a not so positive opinion of me.

Not Erik, though. He loved me for who I was; teenage mistakes and all.

I shook my head at his question. "No, babe. In a good way. Pick me up."

His grasp became more sure as my feet left the floor. As I rose in the air, it became more obvious to me that this would become my main transportation if I continued shrinking.

"How are you doing?" he asked, standing up fully. "Being picked up as weird as you thought?"

I couldn't remember the last time someone had picked me up, let alone like this. Even my mother hadn't carried me around from what I could remember. Hell, I had been five and a half feet tall by the time I finished elementary school. I gave Erik what I hoped was an encouraging smile.

"It's weird, but kind of okay."

He nodded. "Kind of okay. I can deal with that." He then situated me on the nook of his arm so that I could drape my legs towards his stomach. "Is this okay?"

"I wish you had handholds," I answered before wiggling my dangling toes. The whole situation was very strange, but not terrible.

He lifted my chin with his finger, bringing my face to meet his. For the first time in months I was able to look directly in his face without almost breaking my neck. I had missed these moments more than anything. His face moved closer and his lips touched mine.

"Still okay?" he asked, eyes nearly crossing as he pulled away.

God, he was beautiful.

My heart sank. It wasn't fair that I had somehow ended up with such a wonderful man and now such strange circumstances were pulling me away from him. He was still there. He held me. He kissed me.

"Really okay," I said before I wrapped my arms around his neck. "You know I love you, right?" I pressed my face between his neck and collarbone.

He kissed me on the cheek. "I think I have an idea."

In a few weeks we'd be leaving our apartment.

Already I felt sick thinking about it, but feeling Erik's strong heartbeat and the gentle caress of his thumb against my hip gave me comfort. I still felt strange about making him go through this. Not every man would do this. Not every man would stick around for something so bizarre. But here he was. I smiled at the thought, wondering what I had done so right to receive a man like him, and what I had done so wrong to be losing it all like this.

"Do you mind if we call my parents?" he asked, resting a hand on my shoulder and breaking my concentration.

"Weren't you just talking to them?" I dared to smile. "In fact, wasn't that how this whole thing started?"

"I hate to break it to you, Lils, but when they call, they're not just looking to talk to me and see my handsome face on the computer screen. They like you too, Lils. I can't tell you how much it would mean to them if you talked to them. Especially with everything they've done for us."

"I know," I muttered. "You're right."

"It doesn't have to be anything exciting. Just see them. Let them see you. Just once."

I nodded bravely. With everything Erik had done for me so far . . . I owed him so much more than a simple Skype call to his mom and dad. But it was a start. I smiled up at him.

"I guess your mug can't be the only they see when they call."

Six

27 Inches / 2 feet, 3 Inches

"**N**O STAIRS. THAT'S a plus, right Lils?" Erik's voice sounded hopeful as the car came to a stop and he removed the keys from the ignition. "Looks like a pretty normal-sized home to me."

"I can't see over the dash," I muttered.

"Oh! Right." He shot a smile in my direction before he jumped out of the car and rounded to my side in what probably only took him a few long strides.

The door popped open before I chance to open it myself and I slid off of the passenger seat, hopped down, and took in the remoteness of our new home. Trees cluttered the area, creating a sort of 'gingerbread house' type feel, and there was something sad and lonely about the property as well. It was extremely generous of Erik's parents to rent us out a place this remote, but somehow still modern, but at barely two feet tall, anything "normal-sized" seemed pretty intimidating. As I leaned my shoulder against the door to close it, Erik shifted closer.

"Don't worry about that," he said, closing the door with a crooked grin. "I can do that kind of stuff for you, Lils."

"It's a door," I muttered. "I'm not helpless; I can shut a car door."

His face flushed. "I know you're not helpless. I just want to help out when I can."

I turned away from him, trying not to show my annoyance. I still wanted some independence, and I had to remember what this must be like for Erik. I stared up at Erik and gave him the best smile I could manage. It was hard to look up at him. Not only did it hurt my neck . . . my stomach would have a strange, terrible hiccup lately as I took him in standing so far above me.

I tried my best to ignore it and turned my attention back towards the cabin.

"It really is amazing that your parents are letting you do this. Not many people our age have the option of not working."

He shook his head. "I would have taken out a loan if I had to. You were the one who said you wanted me around more, and honestly, Lils I wanted that, too. I hated waking up every day knowing that you would have to spend the day alone in that house. I felt terrible."

"You did?"

"I really did. It was so hard for the last few days there. Life just kept pushing forward like everything was normal. It was hard to put on a smile knowing what I knew." He crouched down to be near me. "Now I can finally be a proper husband. You won't have to worry about a thing."

I tried not to frown. I knew what Erik was trying to say, but the way he said it almost sounded like he was preparing to take care of an invalid. "I'll have plenty of things to worry about. I mean, living out here we can't order food every day."

"I can cook."

"And even though it's only the two of us, we will get the house pretty messy."

"I can clean."

"And laundry . . ."

"Got it."

"And the dishes."

"Okay."

"Erik!"

"What?"

"I don't want you to think of yourself as my personal maid or anything like that. I'm still perfectly capable of doing all of those things. I don't want to spend the rest of my life—or whatever's left of it—sitting around and watching movies. This is already hard enough, but I don't want you to feel like you have to serve me—"

"I want to. Lils, I don't mean to sound like a spoiled brat, but it's not like I had to do a lot of those things growing up. I really don't mind now, especially if it will make your life easier."

"I can't—" I started, but Erik playfully muffled my complaints with his hand.

"Damn Lily," he grinned. "You really are going to fight me about this, aren't you?"

I pushed his hand away and to my relief he allowed me to do so. "You're damn right I'm going to fight you. I'm not going to just sit around on my ass for no reason."

"I think that you have a pretty good reason—"

"Challenge me, Mr. Larkin."

His dark eyebrow arched. "Challenge you?" He repeated, familiar with the game.

We would often challenge each other to try new things. At first, the game was mostly for me so Erik would have an excuse to make me try new things. Stuff like eel sushi and vacuuming the apartment more than once a month. I hoped that what was happening to me wouldn't take away Erik's competitive spirit. When a smirk appeared on his face, I could see that he was game.

"Did you have something in mind, Mrs. Larkin?"

"You say I can't do things like cooking and cleaning. I'm telling you I still can. I'm short, but that will not make me useless."

"I never said you were useless—"

"What would you like for dinner?"

His attention shifted towards the cabin. "I really don't think there are a lot of things in the house yet, Lils. Maybe I can see if somewhere will deliver Chinese food or pizza."

"No. I want to make something." I kept my voice firm. "What's in the house?"

Erik knitted his brows together before he snapped his fingers. I flinched at the noise, and firmly stood my ground in a child-sized dress with straps threatening to fall off my slender shoulders. I angrily pulled them up, still waiting to hear Erik's idea.

"Spaghetti." He smiled wickedly.

"Spaghetti?"

"Uh huh. The stuff should be here. Pasta, sauce, onions, garlic, maybe even some parm in the freezer. My parents love spaghetti. I don't think it will be that hard."

"I don't care if it's hard or not!"

"Fine, Lily," Erik said, leaning closer to me. "How about this? Spaghetti is what I want for dinner. Will you please make it for me?"

I tried to smirk. "Such a bossy husband, you are. If you insist. Challenge accepted," I said casually.

"Get to it, then," Erik said, unfolding himself into a standing position.

I tilted my head way back, and when our eyes finally met he looked incredibly sheepish.

"God, you're so small now," he muttered. "How about . . . um . . . I give you a hand?"

My face reddened. "That won't be necessary. I still have legs. I can walk."

"Well, if you're sure . . . I mean, I don't mind carrying you."

"I'm not a kid, Erik!"

I stormed past him towards the front door. His footfalls landed with gentle thuds behind me, but I didn't turn. Lately, there were times when Erik would look at me, so confused and so desperate that it took the air right out of me. Kindness was one thing, but when it felt like pity or concern, I couldn't handle it.

When I finally reached the front door, I realized that I didn't have the key. Erik's shoes grated the cobblestone pathway and my heart hammered as he grew closer. Why was my body reacting this way to him?

My palms grew clammy and as stopped beside me, and my breathing became ragged and forced. With horror, I realized my body was warning me not to trust something so much bigger than itself. *Run. Run away and run fast. Don't turn back.*

I was afraid of my husband.

"Are you okay?" Erik asked from far above my head.

I couldn't look up at him. He'd know what was wrong the moment he saw my face. "Why wouldn't I be okay?"

"You're . . . you're shaking." He reached out and took my hand between his fingers and thumb. "What's wrong? You're . . ."

His eyes widened with a strange expression that I couldn't quite decipher. He pieced together my expression with the accuracy of today's top psychiatrists.

"You're not scared of me, are you?"

I tore my hand away and sheepishly rubbed my arm. "Don't be stupid," I said to the welcome mat.

"You are. Otherwise, why would you shake like that?"

"Maybe because it's cold."

"It's nearly summer."

"It's getting dark."

"Lily."

"Erik."

He sucked in a breath. "Fine then. Keep everything inside. Don't tell me what you're feeling. That's fine. I'll guess—but I warn you—I'll probably guess wrong if you don't talk to me." He stood up, unlocked the door and stepped inside.

Noiselessly, I followed him as he strode into the family room, and plopped himself on the couch.

"Are you mad at me?" I asked.

He leaned back on the couch, his head hanging over the back with hair that was much in need of a trim falling behind him. "No. I'm trying to remember that, size change or not, you're still you."

"What's that supposed to mean?" I asked, frowning.

He continued to stare at the ceiling. Fancy dark wooden beams couldn't bring a warmth to this place yet.

"It means you still keep secrets from me. I don't usually mind; in fact I think it's cool that you always want to be your own woman and be strong for both of us. But this is a little different. You have to recognize that you're going to need help. You're going to have to accept that you need me." He paused. "That we need each other if we're going to have any chance of getting through this."

"I understand that—"

"*No*. I really don't think you do. Whatever. I understand it. If you want to try and make dinner on your own, go ahead, Lils. I'll be right here."

I didn't reply. He was obviously upset, but I couldn't help my reaction. I didn't want to be useless. If I couldn't help him, what was the point of him staying with me? What was I good for?

Erik continued to stare at the ceiling until finally his eyes closed. He was done arguing, but I wasn't done fighting.

I could do this. I was still me. I could cook.

I determinedly turned towards the kitchen and left Erik to relax. How impressed would he be if I could make us dinner without help? What would his reaction be if he woke up and all the places were set and a heaping bowl of spaghetti waited for him?

I did a quick once over of the modern kitchen.

Stove. Check.

Pasta? I walked up to the closest cabinet and pulled it open. Check. Bottom shelf. What a relief! I wrestled the large box onto the floor. Surely Erik wouldn't mind ziti pasta instead of regular spaghetti. I set the box down on the ground and looked for a stepping stool. I had to get the pasta sauce next. Erik or his parents must have prepared the house for me because there was a small ladder set up in the kitchen.

Great.

I had to say, I was pretty proud of myself so far! It was almost sad that such a menial task was something to celebrate at this point, but I tried to press on.

"Onions and garlic," I muttered next, trying to remember the ingredients that Erik had listed. Erik couldn't stand the flavor of plain spaghetti sauce out of a jar and insisted we always cook onions and garlic with it, but I wondered how I was supposed to chop an onion or mince garlic without killing myself. I glanced toward the living room and wondered how upset he would get if I didn't take this extra step.

I frowned. He'd be okay with it.

Violently, I shook my head. No, I refused to cut corners. I pushed the ladder next to the kitchen island and, with great effort, managed to hoist the sauce and the pasta step by step to the countertop. When I had crawled onto the counter I noticed a three-tiered bowl filled with onions, shallots and garlic bulbs. I sighed in relief. I didn't have it in me for a full-kitchen search.

"Time to get to work," I said to the bowl of onions.

I took a small onion out and stared at it. It was larger than I had thought.

Then I took in the fresh garlic bulbs.

Then I thought about getting a pot out of the cabinet, filling it with water, and bringing it to a boil.

All these impossible tasks seemed to bombard me at once.

Maybe I couldn't do this by myself.

Erik was in the next room, and he was more than willing to help . . . no. Not yet. I wanted to show him that I wasn't useless.

A bead of sweat formed at my hairline and I angrily brushed it away.

I would not be useless. I was still a human. A small human, but I had not lost my humanity yet. One step at a time.

After a few more minutes, and a great amount of effort, I retrieved the smallest serrated knife from the knife block and drug it down the counter to the cutting board. Erik began to stir, so I had to show I was hard at work. I grabbed the onion, held it steady with one hand, and began to saw at it with my cartoonishly large sword.

The smell of the fresh onion stung my eyes and I gasped. I often teared up when I sliced onions, but this time I was practically blind within a second. The smell was so strong—stronger than any other I had cut before.

"Come on," I muttered. "You're just an onion! What are you, some kind of Hulk onion?" I grumbled while still sawing away. I sniffed and tried to blink away the tears, but they were a torrent.

I couldn't even make my husband a damn spaghetti dinner! It was too much! I'd barely even started and already I was having troubles. I turned my back on the onion, let the knife fall on the board with a dull thud with burning tears still streaming down my face.

"Do you want help now?"

Startled, I turned quickly and Erik's blurry outline stood in front of the kitchen island.

"Don't make fun of me."

"Wasn't gonna."

"I'm only crying because of these stupid onions." I went to wipe my eyes.

"Don't do that!" Erik shouted, quickly reaching over to snatch my hand. Terror struck my heart before his voice came. "I mean, don't rub your eyes while you have onion juice all over them, Lils," he said gently. "You know better. Let me take you over to the sink so you can wash them."

"I can do it myself," I began to mutter as Erik's hands suddenly swept me off the counter.

"Oh, for God's sake," he said, holding me close. "I can't believe you're being so proud." He walked me over to the sink, turned on the water, testing the temperature before he leaned over. "Go ahead. Use soap."

"I'm not a kid—"

"Is there an echo in this house, or is it just me?" Erik interrupted. "I know that, Lily, and for the record I'd say the same thing if you were still six feet tall, so I don't want to hear it."

I washed my hands, allowing the cucumber melon scented lather to build between my fingers before I rinsed them off.

"It really wasn't a big deal," I said. "I would have gotten it done. It would have taken some time, but I could have done it."

"Is me knowing that good enough for you?" Erik asked as he walked back to the kitchen island. He set me down on the barstool and leaned against the counter.

I staggered back a few inches. "Excuse me?"

"Is my knowing that you can do these things yourself going to get you to stop this behavior?"

"What behavior?"

"Lils, please don't play dumb with me."

I bit my lower lip. "What do you want me to say, Erik? I want to help."

"I get that. Now, can you understand that I want to help?"

I shrugged.

"Lils," Erik said firmly. My chin arched to meet his gaze. "Please try to get this through that thick, tiny skull of yours. You don't have to face every obstacle alone. I'm here for you. I'm your husband."

"I don't want to rely on you so much. I'm tired of you giving me things and I can't give you anything in return." I shrugged. "At least not anymore."

"You think chopping onions and garlic is that important to me? Come on, babe. What matters is us staying together. As a team." His finger dipped under my chin, pulling my attention to him. "Us learning to rely on each other. You're not alone—not as long as I'm around. You have to realize that you need help sometimes. And that I, as your husband, want to give you that help."

"I feel so helpless already."

"Then talk to me about it instead of lugging around a jar of pasta sauce like it's a keg of beer for a frat party." His face changed slightly. "How did you manage to carry that thing out of the cabinet anyway?"

I smirked. "Don't underestimate me."

"Remind me not to." He let out a low whistle, pulling his hand away. "I have to ask, though . . ."

"Oh God, what is it?"

He sheepishly rubbed the back of his neck. "Uh," he reached over and grabbed the jar. "How exactly were you planning on getting this open?"

My face dropped. I hadn't even considered such a thing. "Well, I'm sure I would have figured something out!" I blurted with red cheeks. "I'm pretty tough."

"I have no doubts about that, but these things can be hard to open even when you're . . . my size."

"Which I'm not anymore," I mumbled.

"Which you're not. And we have to accept that."

Reluctantly, I nodded. "Consider it accepted, and not liked."

"Good enough." Erik easily unscrewed the jar, placed it on the counter, and then reached for the knife. "Now. Will you allow me to take over, or is this going to be a federal case? Should I call my dad?"

"It's not going to be a federal case, but isn't there anything I can do to help you anymore?"

"Well . . ." Erik said slowly with an exaggerated thinking motion. "I guess there is something you can do for me."

"Oh?" I perked up slightly. "What's that?"

He leaned over. "Give me a kiss."

I blushed and quickly turned away. "Don't be dumb. That's not what I meant, moron."

"Why am I a moron? You're my wife, and I want a kiss from my wife."

I pressed my lips together into a thin line. "It's different now."

"How's it different?"

"I'm like a child to you. A doll."

"I swear to God. We're going to have to play a drinking game where you take a sip of beer every time you say the word child or kid to me. You'll be piss drunk in an hour. Dammit, Lils, you are *never* going to be a child to me. I could never see you that way."

He pulled me off the counter and held me against him. I found no way to wriggle out.

"Is kissing me so terrible now?" he asked with a trace of vulnerability.

I couldn't answer him at first and his face found its way to fill up my vision.

"Lils, *is* it terrible?"

I stopped squirming and willed my body to stop screaming that I was in danger.

The man before me was still Erik. My Erik. My husband. Same

light blue eyes. Same jet black hair. Same scruffy chin. I shut off the part of my brain that wanted to squirm and escape as I leaned forward, took his cheeks in my hands and pressed my lips against his.

Speaking of familiar, he still smelled like citrus and grass.

"See?" Erik pressed me closer.

I wanted to melt inside of him. "See what?"

"This isn't so bad, right? Kissing me?"

I smiled into his lips. "Not so bad."

He pulled my mouth to his, awkwardly molding his kisses into a much tinier target. I didn't resist. I wanted these moments.

After all, they couldn't last forever.

Seven

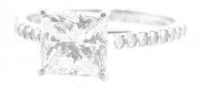

18 INCHES / 1 FOOT, 6 INCHES

AN UNFAMILIAR SENSATION poked me hard in the side, so, with a groan, I turned away.

I wasn't in the mood to deal with anyone. Especially not Erik. It was a cruel thing to say, but with how small I had become I was having a terrible time adjusting. Erik had managed to treat me as well as he could, but everything pissed me off lately. If I could keep control of Erik then somehow, I could control myself. And if I couldn't control him, I was as good as gone.

I was losing my humanity, and I wanted control of something. The only thing I could control now was Erik.

Him and that damn fat squirrel I saw at the window a few days ago.

The jab to my ribs came a second time.

"Come on, Erik," I mumbled sleepily. "Leave me alone." I tried to push the large object away.

"She sleeps a lot more now." Erik said from someplace far

above my ahead.

"Mmmmm. I wonder why that is? Perhaps her body is tired from the constant changes?"

Two voices.

I pinched my eyes shut and hoped I was dreaming. No one else was supposed to be in this house. I had told Erik that I didn't want to see anyone anymore, the voices continued. Erik must have caved and brought someone over. Whoever it was, they were *both*. I decided to keep pretend sleeping in hopes that they would grow bored and leave.

Like anyone would grow bored with a woman under two feet tall sleeping helplessly below them.

"Lily?" Erik tried. "Lils, wake up. We have a guest."

So there was someone else.

"Not a guest so much as a concerned friend."

Recognition struck my features behind closed eyes and open ears. "Mark?" I rolled over. The doctor buddy himself hunched over the couch with Erik. I quickly sat up. "Mark?" I squeaked, backing away. "What . . . what are you doing here? What were you doing?"

"Now, now, calm down," Mark said, holding up his hands with a slightly sad expression. "I was worried about you guys, so I asked Erik if there was any way that I could come and visit you."

"So . . . what?" I asked, turning to Erik. "Don't you think this is something we should have talked about?"

Erik glanced away. "I was sure you'd say no."

"I told you I didn't want *anyone* to see me like this, so of course I would say no."

"Lily, you can't totally blame Erik," Mark offered in that soft 'doctor-y' voice of his. "I've been asking him about this for some time. I can't help being curious."

I narrowed my eyes at the two grown men hovering over me. "Curious?"

"Yes. Merely curious—"

"I'm not going to leave with you and allow you to perform tests on me or something like that. You know that, right? I'm here because I'm trying to stay away from this kind of exposure." I grew nervous. It wasn't as if I could stop them. "I'm not leaving this house."

Mark light eyebrows shot up into his even lighter hair. "What? Are you kidding?" He blurted, turning towards Erik. "She's kidding, right?"

"She's probably not kidding."

"Oh," Mark said, slowly pulling away from the couch as he spoke towards the curtained-off window. "I'm sure you must know, deep down, that I would never do anything like that, Lily. I really have been worried about you." He shook his head before he turned back around and settled himself on a nearby chair.

Erik sat next to me. I slid to the end of the couch and let my legs dangle over the side. I felt nervous with both of them sitting so close. Even Erik, who I loved and trusted, made me feel awkward as he loomed next to me. We were no longer equals.

Mark cleared his throat. "How are you feeling?"

"Less than human," I muttered. "How the hell do you think I feel?"

"Lily," Erik said gently, glancing down. "Mark's here to help."

"Help how?" I shot back and turned to Mark. "You're here to help me, are you? How are you going to help? Have you found something to stop the shrinking?"

He blustered. "Well no, of course not—"

"Can you get me back to my original height?" I challenged.

"No, Lily—"

"Well then what *are* you going to do?"

"Lils," Erik cut in before I could get myself any more riled up, "Mark's worried that you might be becoming depressed. You remember, like before? Before we started—"

"*That's* what this is about?" I shouted. "You're worried that I'm becoming depressed?"

"Well, Erik had mentioned . . ." Mark began.

I snorted. "I'm sure he did. Look, I'm not taking anything! Do you not see *this*?" I motioned to my body. "Would you actually try to medicate me?"

"No, but it might be a good idea to talk to someone else—"

"I've never heard of anything so stupid in my life! Is this some sort of a joke? Or is this really the best you guys could come up with so you could have your little bromance?"

"Lily, that's not the only reason I'm here," Mark continued.

"It's not?" Suspicion dripped from my accusing tone.

"No, of course not. It was only a suggestion, but since you are so against it—"

"I am," I practically growled. "What the hell else do you want other than to try pumping me full of drugs?"

"Lily!" Erik's voice thundered.

I winced and clapped my hands over my ears. "Ouch?"

"Eh, sorry," Erik said, lowering his voice. He reached his hand out to take mine.

I pulled away before he had the chance. I refused to look at him and focused on Mark instead. "So what? If you're not here to put me on medication, or have a Dr. Phil moment, then what the hell else could you have to tell me?"

"I wanted to discuss your condition." Mark began slowly as he leaned back in his chair. "This whole situation has got me wondering."

"Wondering what?" Erik asked.

"To start, I wondered how such a thing was even possible. It seems so unbelievably likely. Was it possible that such a thing happened before and somehow skipped the medical literature?" Mark turned his attention closely to me. "I don't, or rather, I can't believe that you are the only one who has ever gone through something like this."

My bad mood evaporated at these words. This was certainly not what I was expecting Mark to say. I had hoped that I wasn't the only one—I refused to believe that I was going through something like this alone. "Do you really think there's others out there?"

Mark nodded. "Yes. I wasn't initially sure how to go about looking into such a thing, but I eventually found some potential clues," he paused for effect. "And I'm almost positive that I'm right."

"You're kidding," Erik hushed. "You're saying there are others out there, humans who are shrinking like this?"

Mark nodded. "It does seem impossible, doesn't it? Human anatomy shrinking goes against everything I've ever known or seen. It goes against science itself, and I believe that for this reason it has been kept a secret from the world. We certainly have had little trouble keeping this under wraps, wouldn't you say?"

Dumbfounded, I nodded. "Why would their doctors keep quiet about it?" I asked. I didn't want to place any ideas in Mark's head, but I wanted to believe his being here proved that his heart and mind were still in a decent place.

Mark pressed his lips into a thin line as he took in Erik and I. "Why indeed? That's what I wanted to know. A medical discovery like this—provided you could prove or explain it—would be the discovery of the decade . . . or the century!"

Erik's hand curled around mine. It was nice to know he was still there for me. I smiled and he sent one my way before returning his attention to his friend.

"Of course I didn't ever think of it that way!" Mark quickly amended. "I'm simply stating that there are other doctors out there who might think of such things. Especially those who aren't close to the family that they are seeing."

"Go on," Erik said.

"Apparently there have been mumblings in the medical community of incidents such as this. Other doctors have posted very um . . . 'non-professional' articles about patients shrinking. Losing six or so inches over the course of a year for no apparent reason. Such a thing is more common than you realize."

"You're kidding," I muttered.

"That's what happened with you at first," Erik said.

"But it never stopped!" I blurted. "I didn't stop at six inches! I kept going!"

"I think it's fair to assume that these patients did as well. Perhaps they stopped seeing the doctor before it became too obvious. I can't imagine that anyone would voluntarily submit to a lifetime of being poked, probed, and gawked at as they became smaller and smaller."

Just the idea of being pinned down to a table like in *Gulliver's Travels* was enough to send a chill up my already stiff spine. "That makes sense. But where do they actually go? And *when* do they stop getting smaller? I've got to be close to the end of this, right?"

"Now, now," Mark said. "I can't say that I know any of that. Remember this is all murmurings that I found on the web. Nothing official has been documented, and as far as I can tell, no doctor wants to admit that they have a 'shrinking' patient who suddenly stopped coming see them."

I frowned. "So no one has stuck with their doctor long enough to allow this to be confirmed?"

"Weren't you just screaming that you would never come back with me if I asked?" Mark reminded me. "Would you leave this house and come back with me so that I could prove to the entire world that humans are capable of shrinking? I mean, I'm sure you'd get your own reality TV show . . ."

"*Mark*," Erik said. "Of course she wouldn't."

"I can answer for myself!" I shouted to the two men. "I course I wouldn't." Erik smirked. "Shut up, idiot," I said as I squeezed his finger.

"It's good to see that you haven't lost your . . . ahem . . . spunk, Lily."

"That she has not," Erik tacked on.

"I was saying, I believe that there are people out there like you who thought the same way. They didn't want to be experimented on, so they left."

"What about their families?" I asked. "Each one of these people has families, friends, or loved ones. They can't disappear off the face of the earth," I paused. "I mean . . . can they?"

Mark bit his lip and ran a hand through his short, sandy blond hair. For a doctor-y rich kid like Erik, it was actually pretty surprising that he wasn't married with kids yet. He wasn't an ugly dude.

"Like I said, there isn't much to go on. The whole thing is very nebulous because there is no verifiable proof. The families aren't saying anything other than anonymous blog posts. They don't want to be celebrities."

"Not even for the money?" I asked with slight hesitation.

"Even if they did want money," Mark continued. "There seems to come a point where things start to . . . change."

"Meaning what?" Erik asked.

Mark fell silent and took to looking at his shoes. Erik and I both leaned closer.

"Meaning what?" Erik repeated. "What exactly starts to happen? I mean, we already know she's shrinking."

"What else can there be?" I couldn't help feeling scared all over again. "Don't tell me I'm going to sprout a tail and start squeaking like a freaking mouse."

"Again, these are anonymous web posting and the like. There are informal notes from doctors, and there also some things here and there about the families, and the ones . . . the ones who are shrinking."

"Stop beating around the bush, Mark," Erik demanded. "What happens?"

"They disappear."

"What?" Erik and I blurted simultaneously.

"What do you mean they disappear? They get that small?" I asked once I was sure that Erik's voice wouldn't cover mine.

"No, no, I don't know anything about that. The smallest individual I found any reference to was approximately one foot tall, and that particular story felt a bit like fiction."

"So what happens?"

Mark shrugged. "Like I said, they disappear."

I remained silent, and Erik's voice rose.

"And you have no idea what happens to them? Their family wakes up one day and they're gone?"

"Not exactly."

"Dammit, Mark. Stop being so damn cryptic," he groaned. "You said you had something important to tell us and now you're stalling. Spit it out."

"I'm getting there—"

"Stop being so blasé when you talk about the possibility of my wife disappearing!" Erik released my hand and shot up to his feet. "You think this is funny? Do you think my wife's life is a damn game to play? This isn't a joke!"

"Erik, calm down!" I screamed from the couch, but Erik was pretty heated at that point.

His bottled-up frustration had the chance to run free, and Mark had no reason to contain it. Erik shot out his hands and grabbed his friend's shoulders and pushed him against the chair. Furniture groaned under their weight. They were both large men, and even if I were still six feet tall, I couldn't have done much to stop them.

"Erik, please relax! He's going to tell us!"

"No! He's being so passive! He always does this! Even now,

he thinks everything is a damn joke!" Erik shook Mark. "Are you enjoying this? I'm surprised you haven't said, 'I told you so' yet. Wouldn't that be wonderful?"

"Erik, stop," Mark said calmly. "Now's not the time. Let me go, you're upset—"

"You're damn right I'm upset! I'm *pissed* because you're the only person I can trust right now and you're acting like some joker. Why don't you tell her what's really going on?"

"I will, if you calm down—"

"This isn't the only time I'm talking about! I mean about Lily and I! Tell her what you used to say about her!" Erik said angrily.

Color drained my face as I realized I had no idea what they were talking about. "Erik—"

"Now's not the time," Mark said over me, trying to push my husband away. "I'm over all that. I thought we were both over this."

"I thought we were too. Until you started pulling this crap on me now. Tell her what you used to say."

"Erik, that won't help anything—" Erik shook him.

"Tell her now."

"What are you two talking about?" I asked. "Mark, what did you used to say about me?"

"It's nothing—" Mark blustered.

"Nothing eh? That's a funny way to word it," Erik said darkly.

"It's been years. I don't even know why you're bring this up now."

"You know why."

"Erik, just stop," I yelled. "No matter what it was, it's in the past."

I had an idea of what Mark was going to say. If Erik thought for one second that I believed his friends had accepted me with open arms from the get go, he underestimated my intelligence. Mark hadn't liked me at first. Most people didn't.

"I don't need to hear about it," I said and sat back down on the couch. "I don't want to hear about it."

Mark must have felt the anger leaving Erik as he loosened his grip. "But Lily . . ."

"I know what your friends used to say about me. I really don't care to hear about it now. What good is it going to do?" I said angrily. "And let him go. You're acting like an idiot."

Erik removed his hands and stood up. He cleared his throat several times as he adjusted the collar of his faded black polo. "I don't know what came over me."

Mark frowned. "It's fine. These are stressful times, that's for sure."

"It wasn't right to take it out on you," Erik muttered. "And Lils is right. It wouldn't change or help anything."

"Indeed," Mark said. "And Lily?"

I looked over at Mark as Erik came to sit next to me, a little farther away this time. I can't say I minded. I didn't like seeing something so big become so upset. "What? Seriously, I don't want to hear about how you felt about me in the past."

"So I won't say it. Just for the record . . . I was stupid, okay? I didn't know you."

I nodded. "Yeah . . . I get that a lot actually."

"I actually mean it." Some of his calm, doctor-y voice evaporated. "I said some really nasty . . . some stuff that I really regret, okay? I won't say it again, because if anyone realizes that the past doesn't matter much right now, it's you."

"Mark—"

"No, it's okay, Erik. I know what he means. And yes, I understand. I forgive you, okay?"

"Thank you."

"It's all in the past. Like my old self."

Erik's lips parted like he wanted to say something, but closed them without a word.

The three of us fell silent as the realization that I would never be my old self was brought to the surface once again. I would never again be the girl that who played flag-football with the boys at barbeques. I would never be able to put Mark or Erik in a head-lock again. I could never play video games, get tattoos, or go into book stores.

Those things were all gone. And thanks to Mark's latest research, it was pretty obvious that they would never come back. I sniffed hard and rubbed my nose into my sleeve.

Well shit.

"The word is that there are people like you living in communities," Mark continued, breaking the silence.

"Communities?" Erik repeated. "Communities of people who shrink?"

"That's what I've gathered from various disjointed accounts, but there is one thing that is pretty consistent. Again, this based off of anonymous internet postings. Apparently once a person starts shrinking, *they* start watching."

"They?" Both Erik's and my voices hitched at the end.

"The ones who have already shrunk."

"So it does stop at some point," Erik said.

Mark nodded. "So it seems. And those people, they apparently watch for others who are like them. They make sure they are safe."

"How can they do that?" I asked.

"I have no idea. It makes me wonder if it's true," Mark said. "I really don't know any more than that."

I nodded. "Thank you, Mark. I appreciate your coming out here to tell me this."

He shrugged, shifting uncomfortably in his seat. It was so rare to find Mark looking out of sorts, but I think Erik's attack had jarred him more than he would ever admit. "No problem, Lily. I mean—despite what I used to say—you and Erik are two of my closest friends. And for some reason . . . you two work really well together. You just fit."

My eyes widened. "Thank you . . ."

"And I can't . . . I hate that I can't see you guys like I used to. I can't imagine how hard it must be. Me being here must have spooked you pretty badly, didn't it?"

I lowered my chin in shame remembering how just a few minutes ago, I had wanted Mark to do nothing more than leave. Spooked. What a terrible way to react to your fellow man. "It wasn't that bad."

"I thought you were going to scream," Mark said. "It kinda made me feel like a monster or something."

"I know that feeling," Erik said.

"I don't mean to," I said in a low voice, trying to catch Erik's eyes. "I really don't mean to act like that."

"It's only natural," Mark said. "I couldn't imagine going through this. But . . ." he trailed off and stood up, ". . . . I don't want to wear out my welcome. I'm still shocked that I was still able to convince Erik to let me come over at all."

"So stay," Erik offered, standing up with him. "We can make you something to eat before you head out. Lils makes a mean spaghetti," he said with a careful grin.

I actually smiled. "Oh shut up! Will you please let that go?"

Mark paused. "You made spaghetti? So what's the big deal, you've always been a good cook."

"Are we still talking about my Lily?" Erik teased.

"Hey, I'm awesome!" Erik smirked at me, remaining silent. I turned my attention back to Mark. "I tried to make it the other day. I was a bit too small," I said sheepishly.

"Oh? Didn't work out, eh?"

"Not exactly," Erik said. "Come on, stay for dinner. We'll tell you all about it, won't we Lils?"

I liked Mark, I really did, but I wanted him to leave. I wanted to think about what he said.

Was it possible that someone was watching me, even now? The thought gave me chills.

There were so many questions that remained unanswered. How long would I shrink for? Would the shrinking ever stop? What happened if it didn't? I tried to give Erik a convincing smile. Even though he wanted to spend time with his friend, he was still hesitant to ask me permission for him to stay a bit longer.

"Sure," I said. "It's fine. I don't mind, Mark."

His doctor bravado dropped for the fourth time. "Really?"

I nodded. "Really, it's fine. Just so long as you don't plan to kidnap me and sell me to science or the circus."

Both men flushed.

"I would never . . ." Mark sputtered. "Ever!"

"I wouldn't give you the chance to try," Erik said.

"Careful, tiger," I said, hoping that Erik wouldn't get all macho again. It was hot—but still kinda terrifying.

"Yeah," Mark said. "Trust me, I'm not looking to fight you. You're freaking crazy right now."

"That's a little harsh don't you think?" Erik asked.

"Says the man who I thought was going to punch my face in only a few minutes ago."

Erik shoved his hands deep into his pockets, glancing in my direction. "Sorry about that. I guess I can be a little protective."

"You've got the right to be, but I want to hear this spaghetti story." His calm shell cracked as he broke out into another disarming smile. "Tell you what, Lils: Do you still like tacos?"

Just the idea of those little corn tortilla presents filled with meat and cheese was enough to make my mouth water. "Who doesn't like tacos? Why? We don't have the stuff to make them here."

Mark shrugged. "You can get anything delivered with the right tip," he said with a smile. "The same kind you always have?"

I smiled back. A real smile this time. "Carnitas with extra sour cream, extra guac and extra cheese?"

"I take it that you can't eat six anymore?"

"I never ate SIX tacos at once!" I yelled. "With the way you guys talk, you'd think I used to be a pig!"

"You were always eating," Mark joked and pulled out his phone. "Erik? Same thing?"

He nodded. "I'll pass on all the extras, but yeah."

"Wimp," I said with a smirk.

"Seriously. I'm having what she's having." Mark disappeared into the next room to make the call.

After he had gone Erik gave me a strange look. "Are you really okay with this?"

"It's not exactly my first choice, but if I really wanted Mark to leave, do you think he'd still be here?"

"It would be pretty hilarious to watch you kick him out." Erik smiled for a moment before his expression darkened and his lips pulled down in the corners. "What about the other thing he said?"

I glanced away. "What other thing?"

"About others . . . like you. Do you think it's possible?"

I spoke without thinking. "I really, really hope so."

"Because I'm not enough, right?" Erik asked slowly.

I jerked my attention back to him. "No . . . no. I don't mean it like that."

"You didn't mean to *say* it like that, but you said it. I get it, though. We . . ." He looked down the hall where Mark spoke into the phone about his personal tipping policy. Erik turned back with a frown. "I . . . I must look so different to you now."

I blinked. There was so much truth in his words. Erik wasn't the same person I had fallen in love with. The person before me was more monument than man. Every movement caused a fluttering in my heart that wasn't all from lust. A flick of the wrist. A rushed step. A lowered voice. Every part of my body wanted me to leave this terrifying being alone. We were no longer the same. Erik was something to be feared.

I couldn't tell him that. Not with his one shot at normalcy just down the hall.

Erik deserved that much . . . and so much more than I could give him anymore.

"Erik, we can talk about this later. Go have fun with Mark."

He arched an eyebrow. "Go *have fun* with him? What am I? Twelve?"

We both laughed uneasily. "Shut up and go. I'll be here. I have some things to think about." I could tell he didn't like my wording.

"Are you sure?"

"I'll talk to you guys when the food gets here. I need to process what Mark said."

He scuffed the toe of his Dr. Marten into the hardwood. "Lily . . ."

"Erik, please go."

Without another word, he nodded and walked away, following Mark to the other room.

I didn't want him to worry about me for a while. I wanted him to be himself: the guy who led a pretty easy life, with his rich friends and his strange wife.

I wanted one of us to feel normal, if only for a few minutes.

Mark and Erik's thunderous laughter easily carried in from the next room, but Erik stayed true to his promise and left me alone with my thoughts. I settled down deeper into the couch to finish my interrupted nap until the food arrived. A prickling sensation ran up my spine every time either of them shifted or moved, but Erik's jovial voice reminded me of better times. Behind closed lids I could pretend that all was alright.

That was still the last time I ever saw Mark.

Eight

12 Inches

GRASS GROWS. TREES grow. Even at the slowest of rates, these often forgotten pieces of nature continued to grow tall and strong. Everything grows. That's how the world works. Human beings start off small, so small that they are almost insignificant, and they grow up with the hope of becoming something bigger, stronger, older and hopefully wiser.

Growing was a natural progression. Growing was natural.

I exhaled and held my hand up to the sky, staring at my fingernails that I had painted black with a sharpie marker. What bothered me was the idea of growing. It wasn't happening to me for some reason. Not anymore. Almost a year had passed since my initial symptoms. Weeks had passed since I had seen another person besides my husband.

I couldn't bear the idea of anyone seeing me now. I was a doll. I was less than a doll.

I was still shrinking.

There was nothing anyone could do to stop the process because no one had had ever seen it before—or if they had—they certainly didn't want to talk about it. I refused to believe that I was alone. I refused to believe that if my husband Erik and his parents were able to keep such a large secret from the rest of the world that there weren't others out there doing the same thing. My doctor and Erik's friend Mark thought the same thing. I couldn't be alone in this. There had to be someone else in the world feeling the same longing, and this same dread.

I balled up the fist that I held in the sky with a bitter taste in my mouth. The idea that I might not be the only person in the world who was going through something like this was reassuring in a way—misery loves company. Don't get me wrong, I wouldn't wish such a fate on my worst enemy. It didn't matter. I was alone. If the shrinking didn't stop perhaps I would shrink down to nothing. And then what?

The thought was terrifying, and I was already so tired of crying.

A year ago I was only a half a foot shorter than my husband. Over the next few months I dwindled to barely over five feet tall. I didn't like it, but I thought that perhaps I could have become used to it. It wasn't like I was the only woman who was that tall; in fact I was somehow still taller than some women. I could still find shoes with decent enough wedges, and though my husband's height made me a little uncomfortable, I think I could have become used to it.

Looking back, I even started to enjoy the way Erik adjusted to the changes. I wondered if Erik would have treated me differently if I would have been five feet tall when we first met. My husband had always treated me with respect, as a friend, as a buddy, and as a woman he could be romantic with, but he never really had treated me with such tenderness. I could take care of myself and I was a tough woman who wanted independence. That was what

I wanted people to think. But there was still some part of me that enjoyed being treated delicately. Being frail was a strange, new feeling, and for a while I learned to enjoy this new side of Erik. The side of him that wanted to protect me and coddle me and make sure I was safe from the rest of the world.

Of course the shrinking didn't stop at five feet. Erik and I continued to watch my height dwindle.

In a few more months I was barely three feet tall. We had to stop going out. Or rather, I begged Erik not to take me out in public. I slowly came to the realization that I now looked like a child. Though he would never say it, my ever-shrinking body continued to puzzle and amaze him. We then made a crucial decision—moving out of the city and into the country where we could have more privacy.

In the past few months Erik gave up so much to help me. He left his job, his friends, his home, and his family to live in a cabin hidden behind willow trees and unpaved roads. At first I told him not to give up these things for me because it didn't make sense. I wanted him to maintain some sort of normalcy in his life, to disregard the fact that the woman he had married was an unsolvable puzzle by medical standards. Erik had refused. He wanted to be there with me and he wanted to make sure I wasn't driven to insanity during my chosen solitary confinement. I wouldn't tell him to his face, but his choice meant the world to me. I didn't have a family to go to. I had quit my job as soon as I found myself several inches shorter; I didn't tell anyone at work what was wrong, I just quit. I was that person who you meet and 'sort of' know for a few years, and then they disappear and you never hear from them again. I was rarely more than a passing acquaintance to anyone.

What happens to those people?

I desperately missed my black skinny jeans and soft, worn flannel shirts. Doll's clothes were my only option. I tugged at the large button on my plaid jumper. Erik was already making arrangements for me to have clothes even smaller than this if it wouldn't stop. Fabric was thick and coarse enough already . . .

Rumbling.

I focused on the sound. What had been subtle sounds in my once-familiar world were now booming and frightening. Erik was approaching now. I could hear him before I could see him.

I pushed away the grass that loomed overhead and sat up so Erik would notice me as he approached. Each tentative step vibrated through my body as he made his way through the yard behind our secluded single-story house. There were no stairs. I was still sleeping in Erik's bed, and something told me that, this too, was going to change.

Pardon my emo, but I hated changes. I hated the fact that it felt like I was losing him. Losing my life.

"Lils?" Erik's voice rumbled overhead.

Couldn't he even see me through the grass anymore?

It was scary to think that without me alerting him of my presence that I may go unnoticed. I wondered, what would really change if I was gone? Erik could have a normal life and pretend that this whole situation was nothing more than a nightmare that he was dragged into. I would gladly have signed the divorce papers if I had anywhere else to go or had a way to sign them without letting other people see me.

More rumbling.

Erik continued to make a slow approach through the back yard.

A ladybug landed on my shoulder. I used to think bugs were disgusting. And now, at this size they seemed less frightening than they had when I was large. I didn't feel human anymore. I felt more like the ladybug that was perched on my shoulder: a small creature that didn't really register to humans as having a life. Bugs were killed with ease and easily forgotten. I really wasn't much bigger than small animals and large insects.

I'd never understood the concept of humanity before this all started. Now I understood it all too well.

"Lils, if you're around, could you please let me know?" Erik's gentle voice fell around me.

"I'm here," I muttered, waiting for his eyes to settle on me. I hated to watch him lower his chin to his chest to take in his surroundings and to locate me.

He was so tall and strong, a giant version of the man I had fallen in love with. His dark hair fanned out around his eyes, almost long enough that he could have put it in a low pony tail. His light blue eyes darted back and forth to find me. I noticed a hint of scruff building on his chin and underneath his nose. I wanted to sigh. From this angle he was like a colossus that was made to be gawked at by lesser beings. If he wanted to ignore them, he could simply lift his chin and look straight ahead.

He was my whole world, while I was becoming nothing in his.

He spotted me.

"There you are. What are you doing this far from the house?"

He crouched down next to me and I took in the sounds of his clothing shifting high above my head. It was pleasant, but a little scary. Resting his hands in the dirt to steady himself, I noticed how easily the ground sank under his weight; I could hear the earth groaning as he rested on his heels.

I shrugged my shoulders, "When I can't see the house, I don't feel like such a freak."

"You're not a freak," he said reassuringly in a gentle tone that would have rivaled Mark's. "It's slowing down, you know. I've measured you almost every day and you're slowing down."

"Oh hurray, I get to hang out at the size of a Barbie," I said sarcastically. "What good is that?"

"You're still you," Erik went on. "You're still my wife."

"I don't feel very 'wife-y' like. I can't do anything anymore. I can't do the dishes, I can't cook—"

"It's not like every relationship has a designated partner designed to complete all of the chores." His eyes focused. "It's really okay."

"No, it's definitely not okay!" I shot back, becoming angry with how calmly he was taking all of this. How would I be if the roles in this crazy situation had been reversed? Erik winced slightly as I found my feet and stood. "I'm sorry, babe. I don't mean to shout at you. I'm—"

"I know," Erik replied and winced at his own choice of words. "I mean, obviously I don't know exactly, but I understand why you're upset."

I glanced towards the house; from there it almost didn't look so terrifyingly large. "I thought this would be over by now." I refused to meet Erik's eyes.

"It's slowing down."

"And that's great. So we prolong the inevitable."

"The inevitable?"

"The inevitable is me continuing to shrink like this. Slowing down or not, it's still happening. I'm turning into nothing. I'm becoming so small that I can't even interact with you. I could disappear and you wouldn't even know where to find me." I finally turned back to him, watching the breeze catch his hair, caressing it softly. "Erik, I don't think this is going to stop."

His jaw tightened. "It will."

"And if it doesn't?"

He bit his lower lip and I wanted to kiss him. I was well aware that Erik was probably as lonely as I was. Physically we were able to do less and less, and this took a heavy toll on both of us. I began to walk towards my husband, his crouching body looming over me and into the sky. This situation would break him before too long and I didn't want to be there when it happened. I wanted him to be able to move on. As much as I wanted him, staying together and pretending everything was okay wasn't healthy for either of us. I couldn't hold on to him simply because I was scared of being alone.

"I want you to let me go." I reached out and touched his knee. There was a strange silence as my fingers failed to grip the thick fabric of his jeans. I waited patiently for a response, and none came. Instead, a drop of liquid fell to his thigh, splashing on his jeans. "Erik?"

"What?" He sniffed loudly.

"Erik, don't cry," I said pathetically.

Both of his eyes were wet. His sadness was now sadness magnified. I couldn't take this broken version of my husband. He used to smile all of the time. He used to be so happy that I couldn't help myself from smiling every time I looked his way. And now he was like this. I made him like this. Just being with me was sucking the life right out of him.

"Erik, don't cry," I scolded him with a broken voice. "If you cry then I'll cry, too."

"I can't help it, Lils," he said as though attempting to compose himself. "I'm sorry that I can't do anything."

"It's not your fault—"

His head jerked up. "I know, but I wish I could do *something*. I'm your husband. I hate that I can't do anything but pretend to understand what you're going through or just pretend that everything's okay when I know that it's not. I want be strong for you. I want to prove that you made the right decision when you married me."

The things that Erik worried about never ceased to amaze me. But it still wasn't fair to keep him. "I know I made the right decision. But I still want you to let me go."

His voice was surprisingly stern. "No."

"Yes."

"I won't let you go, Lils," Erik said. "You're not some animal to be set free. You're a human being. You're my wife."

I shook my head, raking an unsteady hand through my dreadlocks. "I won't be for much longer."

"What does that even mean?"

"It means I can't be anything to you for much longer. You should let me go before this gets any harder. For either of us." I glanced up, hoping that my words were beginning to sink in, but he continued to stare at me with an odd combination of a steely determination and a broken spirit.

He shook his head. "No." His voice shook.

"I can't be your wife much longer, Erik. This isn't fair to you."

"I don't care what's fair." He reached out his hand.

"What are you doing?" I asked as long fingers and a squared palm filled in my vision.

"I want to hold you."

The hand before me brought tingles down my spine. It wasn't right. It wasn't fair.

Erik pressed forward. "I want to hold my wife, Lils. Can you at least let me do that?"

"Will you let me go?" I tried.

"No." Erik took me up by my waist in his hands. "I'll never let go."

I almost smirked as he brought me to his shoulder, "You'll never let go, Jack? You'll never let go?" I said as I pulled him tight.

"Stop watching sappy movies in your free time," Erik said, squeezing me gently.

"What else am I supposed to do? Try a Tough Mudda?"

"I'm not letting you leave."

"There's nothing I can give you at this point, Erik."

"I don't need you to give me anything except yourself."

"Some self. Erik, really, what kind of self am I if I'm only ten inches tall? Or five? Or even smaller than that? I have no self anymore. And even if by some crazy miracle, this shrinking does stop at one point, then what? You have a four or five inch tall doll for a wife? Erik, you need a life. You can't spend the rest of yours taking care of me."

His expression hardened. "Yes I can."

I took a deep breath, inhaling the scent of his faint cologne. He smelled spicy that day, like someone had broiled an orange and I buried my face into his shoulder. I didn't want to leave him, but there wasn't much time where we would be able to hold each other, even like this. Like a father holding a toy to his body. I wasn't even like a child any more.

"I don't want a life without you," Erik said, gently nuzzling his face into mine.

"I don't want a life without you either."

He nodded above me. "Good."

"The time will come when this won't work."

"I don't think so."

"It will. Erik, if I get much smaller than this, I want you to consider it."

"Consider what?"

"Letting me go."

"You can't ask me to do that. Who will watch you? Who will take care of you?"

"No one. That's the point, Erik."

"That doesn't make sense."

"Maybe not, but if I get much smaller than this, you may not even notice when I leave."

"Lils." Erik pulled me away from his shoulder.

We stared at each other and his finger touched my cheek to gently brush away a tear and push my dreads away from my face. I tried to focus on something else, but his hand remained firm so I couldn't turn.

"I will notice when you're gone, so stop saying stupid shit like that. You're going to drive me mad. Whether you're six feet or six inches . . . size makes no difference. I *will* notice when you're gone."

"Erik—"

"Lils," Erik mocked.

"Please consider it, okay? For me? If I get so small that we can't even communicate normally, will you consider it?"

A black eyebrow arched upward. "And how small is that?"

His change in demeanor surprised me. I gave the question some serious thought. What *did* I consider to be the breaking point of our relationship when it came to my shrinking? At what point would I no longer be able to stand being around my husband, or the human race for that matter? I thought back to stories that I read as a teenager and finally came up with what I thought was an appropriate number.

"No smaller than two inches. When I reach there, we agree to go our separate ways."

"Lils. I don't think it will be that easy," he said reluctantly.

"Promise me, Erik," I pleaded. "Promise me you'll let me go if I get any smaller than two inches."

"Will you let this 'leaving' thing go if I promise something as stupid as that?"

"It's not stupid. And, yes. If you promise me this, then I'll drop it for now."

He sighed loudly, pushing my dreadlocks away with a single breath. Strong fingers curled more tightly around my frame.

"Fine. Two inches, and then I will at least *consider* letting you go."

I smiled at this strange and horrifying promise.

"I don't think you'll ever get that small," Erik added quickly. "Besides . . ." he trailed off.

"What?" I asked as a blush formed on his high cheekbones.

"It's not that I incredibly mind you like this." He chuckled and lowered his voice as though embarrassed to continue. "I don't mind you at this size," he whispered.

I tried to hide my surprise. "And you say I'm the one with the fetish?"

He stood up with me in his arms and I gasped at his sudden move. I was about to squeal when I felt his lips touch my cheek.

"You give me much less sass like this."

"Oh, shut it!" I giggled, trying to lighten the somber mood. "I can give you plenty of sass if you're asking for it!"

"And if I am?" Erik lowered his face to mine so our foreheads touched.

I flushed at the closeness, also felt relieved that he was still acting like this. He still saw me as a human. I wasn't a doll to him yet. I reached out and grabbed his face and kept our foreheads close together. We both closed our eyes. Erik remained as still as the tree behind him.

"I love you, Lils."

"And I, you. I love you." I remained still until I could no longer stand than the sad chill in the air and reached out to pinch the tip of his nose.

"Hey!" he blurted pulling his face away.

I laughed out loud as his nose turned a pleasant shade of pink. "I told you I was still able to give you sass."

"That's not sass! That's spousal abuse!" Erik laughed, pulling me close. "I could have you put in jail."

"Yeah, those bars would work really well," I giggled.

It was a light moment as we both laughed and horsed around in our own private world outside the cabin in the middle of the woods. Eventually Erik leaned against a tree, holding me tight in his arms and we both fell asleep under the midday sun. It was peaceful and romantic, but despite the tentative calm that we both enjoyed that afternoon the promise still weighed heavily in my mind.

Later that afternoon as Erik walked back into our home I pulled him even closer to me. I wanted to remember him. His playful blue eyes and wavy black hair. The scent of citrus and freshly mowed grass. How his two front teeth were slightly parted in the middle and were only noticeable when he truly smiled. I didn't want to forget any part of him because I wanted to always remember that at least for now, he was mine. At the same time, I wanted to make sure that he forgot me when I left.

The promise was set now. No going back. And no matter how hard Erik would take it, leaving him was necessary.

Any smaller than two inches, then I would force Erik to let me go.

Leaving him was the only way to be fair to him. To both of us.

Nine

6 Inches / Part I

ERIK WAS RIGHT about one thing: the shrinking was slowing down, but six inches was still surreal. I wanted to ask him how he saw me now though I knew what he would say. Was I still his wife? *Of course I was.* Was I human to him? *Of course I was.* Was I nothing more than a pet? *Of course I wasn't.* Erik always said the right thing, but that didn't stop the questions from pulsing through every fiber in my body. When I was twelve inches, I felt small and still managed to feign confidence.

It had taken almost three months to realize that I had shrunk to half of that meager size. I noticed little things changing at first. My clothes were looser. I no longer felt safe sleeping in the same bed as my husband. Going outside wasn't worth the effort. I didn't enjoy being on the ground anymore. I couldn't stand it. The world that I had once dominated now loomed over and around me.

Had I ever been human sized?

I began to forget what it was like to be human. It was much like how I used to get when I was sick and I forgot what it felt like to be well. The nice things about colds, though, are that they eventually go away.

I rolled on my side and watched my husband's steady breathing from the night stand. He was enormous, but somehow still attractive in my dulling hazel eyes. He had finally cut his dark hair so it wouldn't brush around his eyes, and his eyelashes still fanned beautifully around him, casting a dark shadow beneath. He didn't snore, and at this size I was grateful for that.

Reaching over, I rested my hand on my engagement ring that I kept next to my tiny bed. It was so strange to think that this thing had once fit my finger. For a while I wore the ring as a charm on a necklace, and eventually as a heavy bracelet. For 'fun' sometimes I would wear it on my head like a heavy crown and Erik would chuckle, but his laugh was uneasy. The stone was cold against my fingers and it gave me a chill to think that I would never have the chance to wear it. Even if I stopped growing today, I wondered if this life was really worth living. I was nothing.

Several months had gone by since I made Erik promise me that if I ever shrunk any smaller than two inches that he would let me go. Where I would go I wasn't sure, but the promise didn't seem as scary then. Now, the promise was only four inches away from becoming a reality and I didn't want to go. I wanted Erik with me because I loved him. He was familiar to me and I trusted him. Was two inches really too small to stay with him?

He stirred and I squeaked at the movement.

"Lily?" His voice was soft.

I turned my face away from his as he sat up in bed and my cheeks grew hot as he kept moving. I could feel every movement now. Nothing could escape my senses. I could hear every hair dancing around his ears, and see the creases around his eyes when he would smile at me gently. I turned back around slowly when he stopped moving and his lips twitched as he spoke.

I swallowed hard as he unintentionally loomed. "Yes?"

"Did I wake you?"

It was strange to be the center of attention of something so large. What was even more nerve-wracking was that as much as I felt I was losing my own humanity, Erik was also beginning to lose his to me. I couldn't tell him that, but the smaller I got, the less of a person I saw him as and more of a large object that was kind enough to dote upon me.

I shook my head hard. "No, I was already awake."

His shoulders slacked. "I keep forgetting how loud I must be to you now."

"It's not that bad yet," I answered.

"It was probably pretty bad four feet ago," he said with a trace of sadness in his voice. I couldn't stand to see him look so hurt. This was hurting him in ways that I couldn't understand.

"Eri," I said softly and he leaned in even closer, resting his elbow on the nightstand. "I think you're handling this as well as anyone could. Better in fact."

The tension in his shoulders slacked. "You haven't called me Eri in a long time."

I shrugged. "It seems fitting right now."

"Oh?" He crossed both arms on the night stand and leaned towards my bed, resting his chin on his hands. "And why's that?"

"I'm not sure actually. Calling you Eri feels right."

He smirked. "You're not making any sense, babe."

"No," I answered with a smile, gesturing to my ever shrinking frame. "I'm not making the least bit of sense."

"I didn't mean it like that, Lils."

"Relax, relax. I'm only joking with you."

"I can't get over how small you're becoming," he went on, lowering his voice to a whisper. "Aren't there people out there who would be really into something like this happening?"

I nodded, remembering all too well the stories I used to read in a hidden corner of the internet. "Yes, there are people who love the idea of having a tiny girlfriend."

"Well, you're my wife and honestly . . . I can't say I'm enjoying this. Not so much because of what it's doing to me, but what it's doing to you. You know I still love you, don't you?"

"Of course."

"Lily," Erik's gentle voice rumbled around me.

"What?"

"I know what you're doing."

"No, you don't."

"I know you well enough to know that you can't ever look me in the eye when you're lying to me," he went on quietly.

"I'm not lying."

"Then look at me."

"I'm good right now," I said.

"I still love you," he repeated.

"I know you always do the right thing."

Erik sucked in a breath, "What's that supposed to mean?"

"Nothing."

"Lils, tell me what you mean by that. You are in *no* position to be snarky."

"I'm not being snarky." I shot back, but couldn't help jerking my head around to glare at him. "And what do *you* mean by that?"

To my surprise he smiled. "I think you know what I mean."

"I beat you up when I was small—don't think I can't do it now because I happen to be a few inches shorter than I used to be."

"Your brain must be shrinking if you think that," he said lightly and reached out to touch my dreads.

His finger set my face on fire as he trailed it down my hair and then my face. I didn't understand how he could still be so gentle with me.

"But back to what I was saying. You know I love you, don't you?"

I leaned into his hand as he cupped it around me, the warmth causing my face to darken with a flush. "I do," I finally whispered. "But I don't think you should."

"I still do."

"I know."

"And you still love me, right?"

Our eyes locked. "More than anything."

His fingers curled around in strange embrace. "I want to hold you," he said, barely raising his voice above a dull rumble. "But I'm scared that I'll hurt you."

"Don't be!" I blurted out. He dared to smile. "I mean," I began in a calmer voice. "You've always done so well. I really don't mind. I . . . I want to be held by you."

His eyebrows shot up. "You do?"

I nodded. "Yes. I feel so alone, even with you. I want you to hold me."

"And what if I mess up?"

"You won't, Eri. I trust you."

In that moment, I think my trusting him meant more to Erik than even me loving him. It's easy to love. You can love a pet, you can love a family member who you don't like, and you can love summer days and vanilla milkshakes. Trust is different. You don't trust many things to hold your life in their hands. In that moment, trust was more valuable than love.

And I trusted Erik. I trusted him with me.

Slowly he scooped me up into his hand. I was still big enough that I could let my legs dangle over. He was so sweet in that moment that any worries of either of us losing our humanity went out the door and down the abandoned roads outside the cabin. All I wanted in that moment was to be held, for Erik and me to be husband and wife despite the terrible circumstances.

He brought me closer, somehow lowering his voice even further. "How am I doing?"

"Good," I answered back and gripped his thumb. He pulled me away and carefully laid back on the bed. Gently he tipped me onto his chest and I settled on my stomach. A warm heavy blanket fell over me then—Erik's hand—and carefully he traced his finger up and down my spine.

"Am I still doing okay?" His chest rose and fell with each word.

"You're doing great," I sighed.

As I was about to close my eyes, his finger stopped suddenly and his whole body stiffened.

I shot up, still shocked at how easily my entire world rocked with a simple motion from one person. "What is it?"

"I thought I saw . . ." he trailed off.

"What?" I looked high up at his face, surprised that his eyes were locked on the nearby window in our bedroom. It was strange to see his face so contorted with confusion, especially from such a low angle. "Thought you saw what?"

"For a moment," Erik began slowly, cupping his hand protectively around my body. "I thought I saw someone."

"Someone?"

He shook his head violently. "But that's impossible," he muttered.

"Erik!" I bellowed when his silence followed.

"What?"

"Will you please talk to me?"

His gaze pierced the window. "Another person."

"Who? Mark?" I didn't want to let hope creep up into my voice. Maybe Mark had found something. Maybe he managed to track down an actual case like mine.

"No, I mean another person . . . like you."

My face fell. "Like me?"

"Like your size. Standing on the window sill."

I gasped, "That's impossible."

"That's what I'm saying!" Erik's boomed in my ears. "It couldn't have been."

"No, it couldn't have been." I tried to snuggle up against him. "You must have been seeing things."

"Y-yes . . . I must have. I'm sorry Lils, I didn't mean to freak you out."

"I'm okay," I replied, "but could you . . ."

"Could I what, Lils?"

"Could you kind of go back to what you were doing?" A nervous chuckle reverberated all around me.

"As you wish." He continued to stroke my back gently.

Doll or not, pet or not, I needed human contact. I needed my husband.

How much longer did I have before until I would be so small that I would be forced to live in this world alone?

A new feeling blossomed in my chest that I hadn't felt in months—almost a year.

Hope.

If Erik really had seen . . . *no*. I shook my head. The movement was so slight that Erik didn't even notice. But maybe . . . just maybe my assumptions were proving to be correct. Mark *had* said he had read of it. Deep down, all three of us refused to believe that I was the only person going through something like this. Maybe we were all right. I looked over at the window where Erik had claimed to have seen this little person.

It wasn't possible.

Was it?

Ten

6 Inches / Part II

I T WAS POSSIBLE. There *was* another. Another like me.

I saw him several times over the next few days. He couldn't have been much older than me, and he looked smaller. I first saw him that night when Erik was sleeping. The stranger tapped on the window and our eyes met. When Erik stirred, he fled. I glimpsed him the next morning while Erik's back was turned as he made breakfast and I sat on the table. Most recently I had seen him on the windowsill while Erik was napping on the couch and I sat on the couch's arm. I didn't understand. What was the stranger doing? What did he want?

The man didn't seem interested in interacting with Erik. The stranger would wave and capture my attention, but when I'd wave back and point to my husband, he'd dart away before Erik could see him. I never had wanted to talk to anyone so badly in my entire life. I wanted to hear a voice that didn't strain my ears.

I wanted to look into someone's eyes without craning my neck. A sick and desperate part of me wished it were a smaller version of Erik, if that makes sense. But Erik was still as human as he had been since this whole thing started.

I still loved him, but I couldn't deny that seeing another person like me made me feel like less of an abomination.

After a while, I stopped alerting Erik every time I saw that small man. There was something about Erik's expression that made me uneasy. What was that shifting behind his dulling blue eyes? Jealousy? What did he have to be jealous about? I had a hard time understanding both his motives and the stranger's.

"I don't think he wants you to see him," I said from the kitchen table. Erik kept his back to me, standing in front of the window in our kitchen. His broad shoulders bunched around his neck. I could tell that the tiny stranger was a subject that he would rather not talk about, but I continued. "I tried babe, every time I've seen him, I've tried to motion to you. He runs away."

"Is that such a bad thing?" Erik asked. "I mean, do you really think that there is a little man out there trying to establish contact with you?"

I lowered my eyes. Crumbs looked like misshapen soccer balls. "You make it sound so silly."

"Maybe that's because it is a little silly."

"You were the one who claimed to have seen him first. I had a feeling that I wasn't the only one like this. It makes so much sense now."

"I don't want you to meet him." His normally kind voice carried a hard edge.

"Eri . . ." The words stuck in my throat when he turned around and leaned against the sink. He stared at me with as much authority as he dared to give a woman standing only six inches tall.

"Lils. I don't think it's a good idea."

"You're acting like a jealous boyfriend," I muttered and crossed my arms as well.

"I'm not your boyfriend. I'm your husband."

I licked my lips. "I . . . I know that, babe. I didn't mean it like that. You just don't understand what it's like—"

"That's because you stopped trying to talk to me about it. Before, I couldn't pay you stop talking about it, but now you're obsessed with finding this person."

"I'm not obsessed," I said too quickly. I wanted to talk to him. I had to know if he had once been human-sized.

Ugh, using the term 'human-sized.' That term implied that I no longer saw myself as human. I glanced up at Erik, his size so daunting as he stuffed his hands into his loose jean pockets. I pinched my eyes shut, trying not to imagine being shoved into that exact pocket. Confined in darkness and stuffiness with only a piece of my husband to keep me company. Fear whispered in my ear, demanding to be heard, but I pressed on.

"I have to talk to him," I finally decided upon.

"Why?" Erik's features turned downward. "Am I doing something wrong?"

I almost laughed. "You have a wife who's shrinking into nothing and you're asking if *you're* doing something wrong? Eri, you're fine. It has nothing to do with you."

"I don't have anything to do with you?"

"That's not what I meant and you know it."

The sadness still wouldn't leave his face. "I know I must be pretty scary to you right now."

"You're not!" I quickly blurted, storming up to the edge of the table. "You're not scary to me in the least."

"Really?" His voice dripped with doubt. "You're really not scared of me?"

I frowned as the whispering continued. *Run. Run away. Get away from something so dangerous.*

"Lils?"

"I would be lying if I said I was never actually scared of you, but I'm more scared of what's happening to me," I answered. "And yes, if I was with anyone else, I'd be scared shitless. But I'm not because I'm with you. I love you, Erik. I trust you more than anyone. You're the only person who I can trust now. If I could bottle up my feelings for you, I'd make you get drunk off them every night."

We both flushed. I didn't say things like this very often and Erik knew that, *but those damn sappy romance movies.* They really had done a number on me.

Erik's face softened. Carefully he crossed the kitchen floor so he stood in front of the table. My head instinctively arched backward to maintain some sort of eye contact and Erik's face crumbled, already seeming to forget how I just poured my heart out to him.

"You're so small." His voice cracked as he lowered himself to a crouching position. "I can't begin to tell you how much I hate myself right now."

"Stop."

"I can't—"

"You're being ridiculous," I said, watching as he crossed his arms on the table and buried his face in the self-made cave. For a few moments I wasn't sure what he was doing until the table trembled beneath my feet. His body shook. "Erik?"

"God, Lils. I'm sorry," he said thickly. "I'm so fucking frustrated and sorry," he repeated, sucking in his breath as he cried into his crossed arms.

My heart shattered at the sight. "Erik . . . babe . . . p-please don't cry," I stammered. My own tears threatened. I couldn't watch this large and powerful being look so vulnerable in front of me. My brain and my emotions weren't prepared for it. Erik took in a few gasping breaths, keeping his face away from mine.

"I can't do anything. I'm failing. As your husband, I'm supposed to take care of you. I'm supposed to keep you happy."

"And you are! You really are."

He shook his head violently, inhaling another painful gasp of air. "No. I'm not. I can't be what you need right now. Or ever. I don't know any more. You're hurting. I see that. You need someone else."

"I don't—"

His large face jerked up from his arms and huge sapphire eyes locked on me. The movement was so fast, so unexpected that I stumbled backwards, landing not too graciously on my ass. He sniffed, the tears falling around his cheeks and chin.

"You do. You really do."

I didn't bother standing; the sight of my husband crying was too much. "I have to know what's happening to me. Maybe he knows something."

"And what if he doesn't?"

I blinked, unsure what part of my husband to focus on. "What do you mean?"

"I mean, what if he's in no different a position than you? Maybe even he doesn't know why this is happening to him either. What will you do once you've found someone . . . more like you?"

"What do you mean, what will I do? What do you think I will do?"

"I think you'd leave with him." Erik lowered his face back into his arms. "I know you're looking for any chance to leave me. First it was that stupid promise, and now this." Annoyance flickered across his tired and sunken features. "I wish I never saw anything."

"But you did."

"I know that, Lils. I only wish I hadn't."

I bit my lower lip and finally stood. "I would never leave with him." I waited for Erik to lift up his head.

"You wouldn't?" he asked into the table.

"Of course not, you're my husband."

"But the promise—"

"I'm not two inches yet. I'm still six, last time we checked."

He shrugged.

"Erik," I said sharply, stepping closer to him.

"What?"

"Look at me," I commanded.

"What for?"

"*Look at me.* I want to look at you." I stepped even closer to the mass of hair and skin that was Erik.

He finally lifted his head. Even as large as he was, I could still appreciate his beauty. *And it hurt.* I didn't want to get any smaller. I didn't want my husband to break down. He wasn't supposed to feel helpless. I stepped up and rested my hand on his nose. He sighed deeply, obviously enjoying the contact. I smiled.

"I'm not leaving you. Not now, and especially not with some mystery man who may not even exist. Who knows? Maybe I imagined him. Maybe the shrinking has finally driven me mad."

He sniffed, his nose twitching under my hand. It was an odd, almost indescribable sensation. He tried to smile.

"You're not going mad," he muttered. "I . . . I can't understand what you must be feeling, but I feel helpless too. I want to help. I want to make this better. God, now I sound like the broken record. And you're too small to do a drinking game."

A small smile came to my face without permission. "Vodka in a thimble probably isn't a good idea right now."

"Tell me about it."

"And besides . . . it's like you said earlier. I know you want to help," I whispered, "and that's enough."

He pulled a hand out from under his chin and curled it around my body. With infinite slowness and care he brought me to his cheek. The warmth, his stubble, everything enveloped me. I fell in love with him all over again. I thought I loved Erik Larkin before, but I never, ever felt like I did right then pressed against his face.

"I'd never leave you for anyone," I said, pressing my forehead to his warm skin.

"That's good," he answered, keeping his voice as soft as mine.

"Yes, that *is* quite interesting."

This voice was not Erik's and I jumped away in shock, moving my mouth without words.

"You!" Erik shouted and quickly snatched me up in his hand, nearly knocking over the kitchen chair as he went to his feet, taking me along for the ride.

His possessiveness in that moment was kind of a turn on.

"What are you doing here? How long have you been here?" he snapped.

A man two or three inches shorter than me stood on the nearby windowsill. He could easily fit through the slightly open window. He was so small. Erik and I were both dumbfounded. He looked surprisingly calm even as Erik strode up to the window with me clutched in a loose fist. Erik must have felt even larger and awkward than before.

"It appears that my presence has been causing a slight disturbance," the tiny man continued, arching his neck back just I did when Erik came close.

"I'll say," Erik grumbled. "You owe me an explanation."

"Consider me an open book. Well, maybe not really—"

"How long have you been watching my wife?"

"Not nearly as long as I have been watching mine," he said. "Well . . . my second wife. I haven't seen my first one in years."

"What do you mean?" I asked in a worried tone. I glanced up at Erik . . . or rather his chin since he seemed to be completely focused on the tiny man on the window sill. "Did she die?"

"Oh no!" Shorty answered, with a chuckle that puzzled both Erik and I. "She's fine—better than me obviously. She's still an Original."

"An Original?" Erik and I asked simultaneously.

"Yes, like your large husband here," Shorty said, motioning to Erik. "That's what we Changed ones call the humans. We're still human, but we are not the original build. Get it?" He smiled, laughing at what I considered the most inappropriate time.

"What the hell are you talking about?" Erik growled.

"Oh yes. My apologies, for bursting into your home without any explanations." The tiny guy cleared his throat and attempted to look more professional if such a thing was possible for a man standing just shy of four inches tall. "I've been sent to make contact with your wife and explain all of her options."

"My options?" I squeaked.

"Yes, obviously you are no longer an Original," the visitor explained.

"I'm still human."

A snort escaped Shorty's lips. "Noun usage aside, wouldn't you like the chance to be with others like you? Isn't that what you have been saying these past few weeks?"

"You were listening to us?" Erik growled.

"Erik, it's okay," I muttered.

"No, it's fine," Shorty said. "He sounds like my first wife."

"Get out of here, she's not going anywhere with you," Erik said.

"I must insist that you let your *Changed* wife decide."

"Come back tomorrow morning." Erik's voice shifted into something more threatening.

Erik's grip tightened and suddenly I felt like a fool for ever wanting to learn more about the short stranger on the window-sill. It was hurting Erik more than I knew.

"You should go," I said. "Come back tomorrow morning as he said. I need to discuss this with my husband."

"As you wish, Lily Larkin," Shorty said, raising his voice enough to reach Erik's ears. I was too stunned by the whole situation to wonder how much he knew about Erik and me. "My name is Sterrin Rosch, by the way."

"Sterrin," I repeated and took in his almost reddish hair and what looked like dark brown eyes. "It's nice to meet you. I hope to speak to you tomorrow."

He nodded. "You have much to learn, Mrs. Larkin. Remember, and this is for you as well, King Kong," he said, staring at my husband. "Once a Changed, it only becomes more difficult to live amongst the Originals."

"What do you mean by that?" Erik started, but the man slipped under the window and leapt from the sill.

Erik was still too stunned to follow him to see how he survived such a plummet to the ground.

"What do you think he meant by that?" Erik asked again.

I shook my head and pretended not to know.

But I did.

Eleven

Six Inches / Part III

"I WANT YOU to go home and see your parents tomorrow," I said to Erik that night as he settled into bed.
"I'll stay and talk to Sterrin."

"No. I'm not going anywhere," Erik answered quickly and
rolled on his side as I settled into my own tiny bed.

If I was honest with myself, I would admit that it was beginning to feel a little larger each day.

"What's to stop you from leaving?"

"I already told you," I said, exasperated that we needed to cover this subject again. "I'm not leaving you. I want to understand
this. If I find out that I'm not alone—"

"You're not alone," Erik replied.

"But I am!" Even with my small voice, he flinched. My
words hung heavily in the air. "I'm sorry," I muttered after a few
moments.

He shook his head. "What do you think he meant when he

said that you had options?" Erik said finally. "Do you really think he's been watching the two of us, waiting for you to shrink until you can't communicate with me anymore? That was kind of what Mark said, wasn't it? He wants to rush in and play the hero who saves you from the big bad giant."

"Come on, we're not starring in *Jack and the Beanstalk*. Sterrin was small and you could hear him okay. Uh . . . couldn't you?"

"Well enough."

Liar. "He was even shorter than me."

Erik pressed his lips together. "Was he taller than two inches?"

I froze. The promise still weighed heavily in his mind.

"I don't think he was quite that small, but he's definitely shorter than I am now."

"That means this isn't over yet."

"Not necessarily, and I'm probably still shrinking."

"It's been days and you haven't gotten smaller."

"I feel smaller though."

"How can you tell?" Erik asked, his puzzled blue eyes settling on my figure.

"You're beginning to seem bigger again." Erik sucked in his breath as I turned my face away from his. "It's not a big deal . . . I'm just telling you how I can tell."

"I see."

"Eri," I pleaded. "Please go see your parents tomorrow. It's been weeks. You must miss them."

He shook his head. "My parents aren't going anywhere."

"I need you to go. I have to talk to him."

"And I need to be hours away from you for that?" Erik challenged.

"I want you to see your parents."

"You want me to give you the chance to leave."

"I thought you trusted me," I muttered.

"You said *you* trusted *me*," Erik corrected. "So trust *me* when I say that I'm not going anywhere."

"What exactly do you think will happen?" I growled. "That I'm going to skip into the sunset with a shrunken married man?"

"He *says* he's married."

"Erik, that's so not the point! Do you understand how much this means to me? I have a chance to have some support in my life other than you. He said he would explain my options! That's all!"

"He also said that living with an Original, or whatever, only gets harder for the Changed, or something like that."

"And I can find out what he meant by that."

"Lils—"

"Erik, *please*! You can't do this. You don't know how much this means to me. You would have had no problems before if I wanted to meet a friend—"

"A guy friend is a little different," Erik interjected.

"If I want to meet with him, I will."

"Lils—"

"No, *listen*," I hissed, hoping that Erik wouldn't try to raise his voice over mine. There was no way my vocal chords could overpower his, no matter how pissed I was or how calm Erik pretended to act. Luckily, he pressed his lips together into a thin line. "It's bad enough I'm shrinking, okay? It's bad enough that I've been going through this alone. And now, finally, when I have the chance to talk to someone like me about how I'm feeling, you're trying to *forbid* me? Are you being serious?"

"It's not like that." His voice sounded so helpless. "I just don't want to lose you."

"And you're not going to." I got out of bed and crossed the nightstand. "Let me put it to you this way. Did you ever stop to think—you colossal idiot—that Sterrin may help us?"

He paused and stared. "What do you mean?"

"Maybe having someone else to talk to will make this whole situation seem less hopeless. I won't feel so alone, Erik. I'll have someone else I can turn to. And you don't have to feel like you always have to be there for me. And also, the fact that I want to talk to someone else doesn't mean I'm looking to replace you."

"I want to protect you. More than anything, I want to know that I can take care of you."

"And you are." I stood on my tip toes and my loose white nightgown draped heavily on the table. "And that's why I need to talk to him. I want to be with you. I don't always want to be bitching, crying, scared, or screaming. I just want to *be* with you."

"That's really all?"

"Yes, I never thought about it any other way. I hate that this is all we can talk about, but I can't think about anything else! I know it's a bother—"

"It's not a bother, Lils," Erik said, reaching out to gently touch my face with the tip of his finger. "It's just hard."

I grabbed his finger, squeezing it tightly. "I know. And that's why I need to learn. I have to learn more about what's happening to me. What could happen to me. For me. For us. Will you let me?"

He pulled his finger away and wrapped his hand around me in a loose hug.

"Is that really what you want?"

I nodded hard, causing him to break out in a gentle smile that almost broke my heart. I hoped that talking to Sterrin was the good idea that I had convinced my husband it was. Truth being, at the rate I was shrinking it wouldn't be long until I hit two inches anyway. I needed options. I hated lying to Erik, but I really hoped talking to Sterrin would make my time with Erik less painful. I wasn't sure how many more days I had left with him so I wanted them to be beautiful.

Even if they were a beautiful nightmare.

"CAN WE SLEEP IN THE same bed tonight?"

For some reason my cheeks grew warm. Several weeks had passed since Erik and I had slept next to each other. Both of us were too nervous about me getting hurt.

I wanted Erik close to me. A prickling sensation that I couldn't quite describe said that I needed him if for nothing else than having a warm body next to mine.

The next day I would find out what the hell was happening to me. If there truly were answers.

Erik's black eyebrow arched. "Really?"

I clasped his finger. "More than anything."

"Okay, babe."

He gently lifted my body towards his. I still couldn't get over how weird it was to be lifted in the hand of someone who I had been only a few inches shorter than a year ago. Erik settled against the headboard and brought me to his chest, letting me settle on my stomach. I immediately felt safe, and fear was a quiet mistress that night. I was completely surrounded by my husband. His warmth, his steady heartbeat, his rhythmic breathing, and the scent of freshly mowed grass and oranges. I reached out and grabbed his starchy white t-shirt.

"Are you better now?"

I nodded hard. "Promise me you'll go see your parents tomorrow."

"Promise me you'll let me measure you before I leave," he said with uncertainty.

I opened my eyes. "Why's that?"

"I think you do feel a little smaller," Erik muttered. "More fragile, I guess."

"I'm still okay."

"I know you are, but promise me—that before I leave—If I decide to leave, that you'll at least let me check how tall you are."

"Eri—"

"Lils," Erik sterling before stroking my back with a single finger. "Let me do this one thing, okay?"

I moaned as his feather-like touch continued to run up and down my back. Erik never had to be gentle before. We used to mock wrestle all the time, and now he touched me with a tenderness and care that I had never before experienced. *Beauty trapped in a bottle of nightmares.*

"I want to take care of you." Erik's breath brushed all around my body. "I'll go home, but I want to know how much smaller you've gotten. Oh! And you also have to promise me one more thing."

"Another promise?"

"Another one"

"What's that?" I asked groggily.

His caresses were putting me to sleep. I felt so safe. Even in this strange situation, I felt at peace with him around me.

"Promise you will be here when I get back."

I smiled. "Moron, of course I will."

Twelve

5 ½ INCHES

"FIVE AND A half," Erik muttered the following morning. He replaced the ruler on the nightstand and we couldn't help frowning at one another.

"I knew it," I mumbled.

"Yeah, me too," Erik admitted. "I don't know how I could tell, it's only a half an inch."

"It means you need to keep your paws off me," I tried to joke. I wanted to lighten the mood. If I gave Erik any indication of how I felt in that moment, he would never leave.

Another half an inch. To a normal-sized person it wasn't such a big deal, but to me . . . I wanted to cry. I had to talk to Sterrin. I had to know what he knew.

Would I stop before two inches? Would this ever stop? What would happen to Erik?

I gulped as Fear answered the question for me.

He'll move on. He'll find someone else to love. He'll finally move on from this horrible situation.

As much as I wanted what was best for him, the thought of Erik with another woman took my breath away. She would probably be nothing like me. I was the polar opposite of my husband. I tried not to think of him with some petite brunette or blond with hair like silk that he could touch and run his fingers through. I tried not to picture him walking around with the nameless hottie wearing a sleeveless shirt without stares or glares.

"Lils?" Erik's voice interrupted my thoughts.

"What?" I answered, trying not to keep my thoughts from overpowering me.

"You okay?"

"Yes. Why wouldn't I be?" I tried to answer cheerfully. "It's only a half an inch."

"I don't actually think you view it that way. Be honest. Do you want me to stay? I'll stay."

"No. You should go home to your parents . . ."

"That was before we figured out you were shrinking again."

"Erik, you should GO," I said, raising my voice. "You should go home, see friends, and see family."

"Alright," Erik sighed and rolled his eyes. "That's it. I'm not going."

"Wait! What?" I squeaked.

"I'm not going home." He palmed his face. "This is so stupid. I can't believe I even considered it for a second."

"Erik. I'm fine."

"No," he answered firmly. "You're not fine. I'm staying with you. I'm not going home so you can talk to this stranger and . . ." he trailed off, involuntarily shuddering. "I'm sorry Lils, but I'm staying here. Sterrin doesn't have to talk to me, but I'm not leaving you alone."

"But your family . . ."

"They will be there."

"And I won't be, right?"

"Lils."

I wanted to fight him, but when I looked into his ice blue eyes that were so worried about me leaving, I found that I didn't have the strength. Dreams of worlds so big that they could no longer be fathomed kept me up night. My muscles ached. My eyes burned. Fear constantly whispered in my ear.

Erik held out his hand. "Come here."

I could still walk, but I couldn't get around without him. I couldn't feel safe without those hands. They had become a separate entity from my husband because he was almost too big to appreciate as a whole. Slowly, I crawled into the warm, spongy platform. He pulled his hand away from the nightstand and brought my body up to his chest. I leaned into him. Citrus and grass. I breathed in deeply as he gently stroked my back with his thumb.

"I'm not going and that's final," he whispered. "I'm not going anywhere."

I nodded. "Alright."

"I hate to ruin this touching moment," a familiar small voice rang out from Erik's open bedroom window.

We both jerked our heads around, startled but not surprised to find Sterrin standing in the window and leaning against the wall with crossed arms.

"You're early," Erik muttered, pulling me closer to the solid wall that was his chest.

He was still gentle, but there was urgency in his touch, an anxiety. My heart raced.

I had the most wonderful husband.

Sterrin shrugged. "You said tomorrow morning. Though I must say I was not expecting to find *you* here." He arched a brow at Erik without the slightest care about their differences in height.

"Is that going to be a problem?" Erik said, standing up and walking towards the window.

I felt like a toy in Erik's hands, pressed against his chest, but there was something incredibly safe about being with him. Despite Sterrin's diminutive size (even by my standards), he felt dangerous. He was something unknown and Erik wasn't taking any chances.

I loved him for that.

"I suppose not," Sterrin relented. "Though I am sure you will not like what I have to say."

"Try me," Erik said threateningly. "You're not taking her away from me."

My skin felt like fire. "Erik!" I blurted.

Sterrin cleared his throat. "Calm down, I am not here to steal your little doll."

"She's not a doll," Erik growled. "She's my wife."

"Ahh yes," Sterrin said with a calm smile that I did not find the least bit comforting. "The Original and the Changed. That fairy tale always ends so well."

My cheeks reddened. Those words sounded like a curse in my ears. They made Erik and I sound like two different species—as if I didn't feel like that already.

"Shut up!" I snapped. That confident little man was really beginning to piss me off. "And what the hell do you know about it?"

"Mrs. Larkin," Sterrin replied. "Look at me. Don't you think I might know more than I care to?"

"Yes," I shouted across the chasm between us. "You mentioned a first wife. That she's an . . . Original?"

"She is. She's with her own kind now."

"Own kind?" I lifted my head towards Erik's impassive face. "We're the same kind."

"At one time," Sterrin patiently explained, "but now you are Changed, and there are others out there like yourself."

"Others?" Erik and I blurted simultaneously.

He lowered his chin. For the first time, his eyebrows pinched together.

"How many others?" he asked carefully.

"Not many. Our diagnosis is rare. I would say there are twenty of us living in these woods. We spread out. We don't need the Originals finding out about us."

"Twenty others?" I breathed. "Like me? There are twenty others out here who are like me?"

"Yes," Sterrin said softly, pity intruding into his demeanor for a moment. "You poor thing. You probably thought you were the only one in the world. We all think that at first—until we're found."

"How?" Erik asked.

"Oh, doctors talk. Our Original wives and husbands talk. The internet has been very helpful. Trust me; our community will learn when an Original is changing."

"And . . ." I paused. "Has every . . . Changed-Original . . . gone with you?"

"There have been exceptions," Sterrin said.

Erik leaned forward. "There have?"

Sterrin nodded. "Yes, some claim . . . that they feel safer with their Original partner. It's rare, but it has happened."

So there was hope that Erik and I could stay together. We were special. We could do this.

"Of course . . ." Sterrin trailed off, "eventually most are forced to seek us out in the end."

"Seek you out?" Erik asked in a low voice.

"It means that becoming a Changed can have different effects. Some of us stop around nine inches, some at six. I myself haven't shrunk for about two years and I'm just shy of four inches. However," his face darkened. "Some don't ever stop."

My face paled. I stared up at Erik who seemed to look as panicked as I felt.

"What do you mean? They keep shrinking down?" Erik said in

a low voice. "For how long?"

"Our community here is one of the taller ones," Sterrin said. "Some Changed folk become too small to feel safe even with us. They move on to smaller communities; we work together but remain separate so no one gets hurt. Speaking of which," Sterrin turned his attention back to me, "you say that you're . . . six inches?" He arched an eyebrow.

"Five and a half," I muttered.

"I see. There is still hope, I suppose. Many stop at four inches. Although for a few—a rare few . . ."

"What?" I asked, leaning forward in Erik's hand. His hammering heart pounded in my ears. "What happens?"

"A rebound effect," Sterrin said.

"Rebound?" Erik repeated.

Sterrin's eyes widened, probably shocked that Erik caught the words. He delicately cleared his throat before he spoke. "Yes, there have been a few who have Changed—"

"That go back to Originals?" I asked breathlessly. Could it be true? As quickly as the smile broke onto my face a sudden snort shattered my growing hopes.

"Surely not!" Sterrin chortled. "This isn't a children's story where you shrink, have fun, and then grow back. Silly girl, if only it were so simple."

"What is it then?" Erik asked sharply.

"Patience, Original," Sterrin replied. "A rebound effect *can* happen. It doesn't happen very often, and no," Sterrin turned his attention to me with a frown, "you will not become an Original. Once you shrink, you are a Changed for life. That's a fact. You will never be near the size of an Original again."

"I see. So this is it?" Erik curled his fingers around me gently as I refused to cry until I was alone.

"Now, now," Sterrin said. "Do not lose faith."

"What *is* the rebound effect?" Erik asked.

I knew that while Erik didn't want to lose me, he was probably starved for any sort of positive information. Time was no longer on our side. If I didn't stop shrinking soon we wouldn't even be able to communicate . . . to exist together . . . I shook the thoughts away.

Sterrin cleared his throat. "Sometimes when a human shrinks and the shrinking becomes too rapid, their body reacts. It sends a chemical that causes their height to rebound. Meaning that you may regain some of the height that you have lost. The height changes usually stop then."

"Have you known anyone who has experienced this?" I asked with doubt.

"Yes," Sterrin said. "I have known four."

"Well, that seems promising. If there are about twenty in your community," Erik said, trying to smile. "That's something positive. That's good news. How tall are they when they get the rebound effect?"

"Often they are around five inches," Sterrin said, "but there is a very fast shrinking which proceeds the rebound effect, and during that time it can be very dangerous to be with an Original."

"What do you mean?" I asked, wiping my nose.

"Meaning," Sterrin went on, "That you may be five and a half inches one day, and wake up the next at half of that! Or shorter! Do you really want to be around *this*," he waved at my husband for effect, "when something like that happens? He may not see you! Assuming that he notices you, he could easily hurt you . . . or worse. I remember a few years ago when I was sent to retrieve a young man when his mother lost track and—"

"I would never do that!" Erik blurted, thankfully ending Sterrin's story before he had a chance to finish. He lowered his chin. "I would never hurt you."

"Not on purpose," Sterrin said bluntly. "You'd be surprised—"

"Not ever!" Erik said angrily. "I'm always watching her. I'm always taking care of her. I love her! Can't you understand that?"

"Of course I can!" Sterrin shot back in a flash of anger which stunned both of us. "I was like you once! Can you Originals not even fathom that?"

Erik pulled away. "Of course I can," he muttered.

"I don't think that you can. Do you think that my Original wife wanted to hurt me? Do you think she simply threw me out with the garbage when I could no longer make love to her? She loved me too. She wanted to take care of me just like you want to do for her." He paused for a moment and his anger gave way to compassion. "It doesn't work. It cannot be. At some point you are going to have to let her go. Your wife is not safe with you and you need to accept that fact, Mr. Larkin. You are dangerous to her. It is a miracle that you haven't seriously injured her already."

"She *is* safe," Erik's voice cracked at the end. "I know I can keep her safe."

"Erik," I said softly. "It's okay."

"Ugh, but here I am holding you at what must look like fifty feet in the air." His usually sharp blue eyes began to lose focus. "He might be right. What if I'm wrong? What if I can't protect you?" He glanced towards Sterrin, his earlier confidence slipping away like dirty bath water down the drain. "She wanted to leave. I scare her . . . I scare my own damn wife."

"It's only natural," Sterrin said with a slight shrug, clearly not moved by Erik's realization. "It's hard to truly feel safe with an Original. It's hard to move on and accept your new life. It is a constant reminder of the life that we once had. What we once were."

"Erik," I started, but he spoke over me without a pause.

"I see how she looks at me. She's so tiny. I try not to scare her, but she's so small and fragile. I could accidently hurt her at any time, and we both know it. I can't . . . I can't stand knowing that I scare her so much and yet . . . I can't live without her."

"Erik, stop!" I reached out and grabbed his shirt, tugging it as hard as I could. "You should go," I said firmly to Sterrin.

"Are you sure?" Sterrin asked.

"I don't mean for forever, but for now, please go. This isn't helping."

"I am here to help you," Sterrin said, "but I mean to be honest."

"I understand that. And I appreciate the information. I still want to be alone with my husband for now."

"Shall I keep watch?" Sterrin offered.

Erik shook his head, snapping out of his trance.

"Keep watch?" Erik asked Sterrin.

"Should I continue to track her diminishing height?" he asked.

"No," I said.

"Yes," Erik spoke over me.

"Erik?" I squeaked.

Sterrin nodded solemnly to my husband. Getting someone like Erik to understand couldn't be easy. I wondered how he got stuck with such an awful job assignment. Maybe he only had it because he was the only one who could stomach it.

"When shall I return, Mr. Larkin?"

Erik frowned, lowering his head and meeting my eyes. I began to cry as reality finally began to set in. This wouldn't work. It couldn't work. The best we could do was enjoy what time we still had together.

"Erik, I—"

"Two inches," Erik said in a quavering voice. He swallowed hard, not wanting to cry in front of the stranger. "Come back when she's two inches tall. That's what she wants."

Sterrin bowed and left silently through the window without another word.

And then the floodgates broke.

Thirteen

4 INCHES

"**I** WANT TO try everything we can," I said with an embarrassed expression. "I don't know how much more time we have. You've seen the measurement, right? It's no longer a matter of if, but when."

"You're so small Lils," Erik whispered. "I'm . . . I'm honestly afraid of hurting you."

"Erik, please." I couldn't help stepping backwards as he leaned in closer. He was so large and close that I couldn't help myself. The look on my husband's face almost broke my heart.

"You're so afraid of me now." He kept his voice low.

Since I only stood four inches, Erik wasn't able to speak in a normal voice anymore. He had to either whisper or speak in a voice so low that it sent rumblings through my entire body. I could understand his trepidation; I was finally beginning to understand what Sterrin meant when he explained that our situation would only become more difficult. Erik was huge—I was barely the size of his fingers—and yet I was the one begging him to not be so scared of hurting me.

Why shouldn't he be scared, though? Anything in this world could hurt me . . . even kill me; the flick of a wrist, a pencil falling, a mouse. More things were becoming obstacles so I spent most of my time on the nightstand next to Erik's bed. He wouldn't allow me to sleep with him because he worried that he might roll on me and accidently kill me.

He was probably right to be worried about that.

"Babe," Erik said softly and held his hand out towards me. "I-I don't know what else we can do. If you would have said four inches to me a few months ago, I would have said I was fine with it, but I never realized how small that really was. I can barely hear you; I can barely interact with you at this point."

"So you . . . don't love me anymore?" I asked, carefully stepping towards that huge hand, so big that I could easily lay across the width of it.

"Of course I love you," Erik said. "I love you so much, but I'm so scared of hurting you. What if I mess up? I don't feel safe holding you. I know you don't want to hear it, but I could easily kill you."

"Pick me up," I demanded, not removing myself from his hand. "Erik, I need you right now more than anything. Ever since Sterrin came, you've been different. You're more hesitant, more scared. Can't you see that I need you?"

His finger twitched and the movement nearly knocked me off of my feet. I gasped involuntarily. That probably didn't help.

"You see what I mean?" Erik muttered shamefully.

"Try to go slow," I offered with a smile that he probably couldn't even make out.

"Lily."

"Erik." I growled back with slight agitation.

His hand began to move, much like an old elevator jerking to life. Gravity pulled me deeper into his hand and I found it hard to believe that I was ever able to hold this exact hand in my own.

We were no longer the same.

He lifted me from the nightstand and settled on the bed, with a large bead of sweat forming on his hairline.

I just wanted a bit more time.

I grabbed the tip of his thumb to steady myself as his face filled up more and more of my vision. At that point Erik was my entire world; the cottage was so big that I couldn't even fathom its size anymore. The only things I could see were Erik's huge light blue eyes, the scruff on his chin and underneath his nose and lips that twitched nervously as he tried to remain focused on the delicate task.

"We can't live like this," I said, still holding the tip of this thumb. "I thought two inches was doable, but four inches is damn near impossible."

"It's like Sterrin said: once Changed, it only gets harder," Erik whispered. "I never thought," his voice cracked. "I never thought it would get this tough. Every movement I make, every time I inhale, all I can think about is you and how my size must make you feel."

I nodded. "You know that we will have to say goodbye soon," I said to him. "You can't keep doing this to yourself. You used to be so happy. You had a life, you had friends—"

"I can still have all of those things . . . I think." He had never doubted us, but it was impossible to deny the reality of our situation.

"You can," I muttered. "You simply can't have them with me anymore."

"You know I love you, Lily."

I nodded. "Sometimes love isn't enough."

"I don't believe that," Erik muttered. His eyes glanced away for only the briefest moment.

"In our case . . . I don't think you have a choice. You and I worked when we were the same. We worked really well, but you didn't sign up for this. We can't feel the same about each other."

"That's not true."

"It is. And even if it's not," I went on sadly, "it doesn't really matter, does it? We can barely communicate. You don't feel safe with me being around and I . . ."

"You don't feel safe either," Erik finished. "I knew it."

"It's only natural for me to feel that way, Erik," I shouted up at him to get his full attention. "Erik, I'm the size of your freaking finger! I'm not human anymore! I'm this!" I motioned to my body and Erik cringed.

"You're right," he mumbled. "You're right."

"I need to be with you right now," I muttered and he leaned in even closer. "I need you to be my husband for these last few days. I need that more than anything, Erik. I don't want to remember us crying, having doubts and being scared of what the next day would bring. I want us to be us in the best way we can."

Erik's demeanor changed. Suddenly his fingers closed around and he brought me to his cheek. His stubble poked me, and even though he still smelled amazing, it was so strong now that I almost had to hold my breath.

Everything about him was too much. It was too much for both of us.

"Lils." His voice rumbled like a gentle thunderstorm. "I know it doesn't mean anything, but I'm so sorry this didn't stop. I'm sorry I couldn't do enough."

"You were perfect," I whispered before kissing his cheek.

"I don't feel so perfect."

"You still are. And one day you'll look back on this like it was a strange dream. The 'girl who disappeared,' is what you'll call it, I think."

"No," Erik muttered. "This is the moment I lost everything.

My love, my wife . . . everything."

"Erik . . ."

"You're right," Erik answered, pulling me away from his face. "I don't want these to be our last memories together."

He finally spoke as though we would never see each other again. It had taken months, but he had accepted the reality of the situation. I didn't know whether to cry with joy or sadness knowing this, so instead I tried to look hopeful. Slowly, he lowered his palm to his chest and I stared up at the underside of his chin before he lowered his face.

"What are you doing?"

"Climb off," he whispered and I obliged, able to remain standing in the folds of his shirt. Carefully he cupped his hand around my body. "Listen."

"What?" He shushed me gently.

"Just listen for a moment."

I fell silent, but he didn't.

Erik's heartbeat filled my ears. His breathing rocked my body up and down in a steady motion. He was a living mountain that was getting farther and farther out of reach. Still, it was intoxicating. I pressed my face into his thin shirt and listened.

I felt him. I felt like I was a part of him.

"You hear it?" Erik asked.

I tilted up my head back. "What?"

"My heart. It's beating only for you. And no matter what the future brings, it will always beat for you."

Tears prickled my eyes. "You're so cheesy," I tried, unable to stop myself from crying. I pressed myself even closer to him. "What will I do without you saying stuff like that?"

He smiled above my head in a place I could no longer reach without his help. "You always call me cheesy, but I mean what I say."

I grabbed his shirt, the tears falling now. "I'm scared, Erik. I'm so scared."

"I know." He leaned back on the bed so I could lie down. His heavy hand settled above my trembling body, pressing me ever so slightly closer to him. "I know."

"I'm so scared," I sobbed loudly. Angrily. Bitterly. "What the hell is going to happen to me now?"

"I don't know, but at least I we both know you can go someplace safe. Because of that, we can hold on to these moments. And we will *always* have these moments, Lily."

I nodded. "God, I love you."

"I love you more."

Erik's hand on top of my body was like a blanket, lulling me to sleep and I finally let my eyes close, losing myself in everything about the man I was about to lose forever.

His scent.

His hands.

His eyes and his words.

His breathing, his heartbeat . . . and his cheesiness.

They wouldn't be mine to cherish much longer. They couldn't be.

WHEN I OPENED MY EYES later I wasn't on Erik's chest. He must have set me back on the nightstand. I couldn't blame him. At four inches . . . safety could no longer be taken for granted. If Erik even doubted for a moment that he couldn't keep me safe, it was best that I stay away from him. Something felt different. I stood up and looked around. I couldn't seem to focus on anything around me. Everything was a strange blur.

"It's happened," someone said from above me.

I jerked around to find Sterrin standing behind me with his arms crossed and a sad frown on his face.

"Sterrin?" I took in a shaky breath and tried to take in the scene. Sterrin was taller than me now. I had to look up to see him. Way up. Something was very, very wrong. "What . . . what the hell happened?"

"Isn't that part obvious? You shrank in your sleep while you were with that Original," he answered and nodded behind me towards the bed. "You're lucky nothing happened."

I gasped, covering my mouth with both hands. "You mean . . ."

Sterrin nodded. "Yeah, you look to be about an inch and a half tall."

I tried not to let the shock register on my face. An inch and a half. I couldn't even make a proper comparison to how small that must be to someone like Erik. Maybe there was something positive. "Does that mean I'm having the rebound effect?" I asked hopefully.

"I'm not sure," Sterrin said. "We should go before he wakes up." He reached forward and gripped my arm.

"What? No! I can't just leave him without saying anything."

"You really think you can explain yourself like this?"

I glanced down, noticing that my clothes had fallen off and I was naked. I quickly grabbed a piece of fabric and covered myself. "Why didn't you say anything?" I hissed.

"Relax, I'm not interested in short women," he said wryly. "Well, not that short. But, Lily, we do have to leave. Erik won't even be able to hear you at your size. Come, we'll get you some clothes and we'll wait to see what happens."

"What about Erik . . ." I tried to comprehend the loud sea of skin and fabric next to the nightstand. It was so vast that I couldn't see it as human.

"I'll come back and explain things to him," Sterrin promised. "For now we must go."

My eyes watered as I allowed Sterrin to scoop me up in his arms like a contrary child.

This was the moment I had always feared. I couldn't even tell him where I was going because I was too small and my voice probably wouldn't have even reached his ears.

Sterrin jumped from the nightstand to a chair rail on the wall and made his way to the window. He ducked out into the pre-dawn mist and made me hang onto his neck as he expertly rappelled down the wall on what appeared to be fishing line. When we reached the bottom, he transferred me back into his arms like a baby. Despite his exertions, he wasn't breathing hard at all.

"I will tell him what happened," Sterrin said gently, breaking my curious thoughts. "He will know that you are alright."

"Is this really alright?" I muttered.

"You are alive, Lily. I would suggest you think about that."

I pressed my lips together. He was right, but I still couldn't stop the tears from falling.

Fourteen

~ERIK~

THE SUN STUNG my skin. I was too used to being inside. Groaning loudly, I uselessly hoped that the pain would go away.

"Ugh, stop messing with me . . ." I muttered, holding up a hand to shield my face. After a moment, something felt wrong. The room was silent. Not even the tiny pitter patter of my wife's feet reached my ears. "Lils?" I felt uncomfortable raising my voice to anything above a whisper. "You okay?"

Silence.

I glanced down, half expecting to find a human-sized speck with dreadlocks on my chest, but my polo was empty. It wouldn't have been that odd for her to move away; she probably didn't want to get hurt. I needed to keep track of her at all times. Inwardly, I cursed myself for falling asleep and leaving her in such a vulnerable position.

Vulnerable. Because of me. My breathing. My shifting. Ugh.

"Lils?" I tried again, eyes darting around the nightstand and bed. "Lils, I can't see you—so can you please let me know where you are so nothing happens?"

Silence. Not even a rustling.

"Lily, please." Panic washed over like someone dousing me in ice cold water. "I need to know if you're okay. Did you shrink? Lily, you only have to shout at me . . . I promise I'll hear you." *I wasn't even sure if that was true,* but I held my breath and listened for a sound, anything that would have caught my attention. A small shriek, her kicking or pushing against me . . . *something.* But I felt nothing and heard even less than that.

She couldn't have.

"Lily." I carefully got out of bed, and lowered myself to the floor to peer underneath. Any movement could seriously injure her, so I couldn't exactly turn the house upside down, but I also couldn't just sit there like a fool! I pressed my face to the cool hardwood floor and called her name. Desperation mounted in my voice.

"Lily . . . Lils! Please, if you fell, if you're hurt . . . if you shrank, I need to know!"

"You won't find her," an annoyingly familiar voice said from above.

I immediately moved into a sitting position, trying to sniff away the tears that were forming in my eyes.

"It would make sense that you're here," I grumbled at Sterrin. I didn't bother getting up. With Sterrin perched on the window sill we were almost at eye level. I tried to keep my cool as anger coursed through me when I saw that annoying know-it-all. "Where is she?"

"Somewhere safe," Sterrin replied.

As if she wasn't safe with me. "I'm her husband," I said sharply. "She should be with me. Bring her back."

"She is no longer safe in your presence—"

"Bullshit!" My cheeks grew hot. "Whatever you did, wherever you took her . . . I won't get pissed if you bring her back to me.

Now."

"She can't be with you right now, Original," Sterrin said calmly. "Even if I did bring her back, it would not benefit either of you."

"And why's that? I'm sure you took her away because she shrunk and that . . . that's fine. She's my wife though—you should have at least let me know!" I felt so helpless sitting in front of a full-grown man who couldn't have been more than four inches tall. He shifted uncomfortably and I couldn't help wondering if he enjoyed this part of the job. Or, more likely, if he hated it.

"You would barely be able to recognize her at this point."

"What does that mean? Of course I'll recognize her."

"At less than two inches tall?"

I sucked in a breath. So she had shrunk.

My eyes raked up and down Sterrin's diminutive form. "How tall are you? You seem pretty small and I'm perfectly able to communicate with you."

"I understand your anger and your resentment towards me," Sterrin said, and I quickly shot to my feet. Sterrin nearly fell off the sill in surprise.

"You cannot begin to understand my anger!" I snapped pointing a finger at him. "You don't know. You don't know how hard this was for me . . . for her . . . for the both of us! Just . . . give her back to me." My voice cracked. "Please."

Sterrin raised an eyebrow, with assumed distaste. It was hard not to feel like an alien under his strange and accusing glare. But I was so out of touch with my emotions, I couldn't control myself. And in his judgmental little eyes, I was simply large, cumbersome, sloppy . . . and dangerous.

"You always seem to conveniently forget that I was once an Original as well."

"So you should understand how I feel! You took her away," I said, trying not to let my voice crack again. I worried that with one wrong look or accusation that he would flee and I would never see him—or my wife again. He was the only connection I had. "When I woke up, she was gone and there was nothing. No note . . . no goodbye . . . what the hell am I supposed to think?"

"I am here." Sterrin answered. "I came to tell you."

"I want to see her," I said, shaking my head. "I don't want to see the messenger, I want to see my wife right now."

"You cannot."

"Why?"

"Because it is too dangerous. Yesterday, four inches was a shock to you. Today, my dear Original, she is only an inch and a half tall! Your voice will only boom in her ears and deafen her. Any movement you make would put her at a great risk. I refuse to allow it."

I licked my lips. I couldn't argue. What was I supposed to do? Pluck up the little guy and dangle him over the toilet until he told me what I wanted? The thought left a nasty taste in my mouth and I shook the image away. "So what now?"

"We wait."

"Wait? Wait for what?"

"The rebound effect. If it happens, that is."

"So you think she has a chance?" I muttered, not wanting to reach for something so dangerous—hope. "You think she could rebound?"

"I told her that I didn't think so, but that was only so she wouldn't hold on to this relationship. But yes, I think she could rebound. She has shrunk quite a bit in a very short amount of time . . . her body may not like it."

"So then . . . I wait?"

Sterrin nodded. "There is nothing else that can be done." He paused before clearing his throat loudly. God, I hated that sound. "Mr. Larkin, your wife is so small that I can pick her up with one hand and sling her over my shoulder like a toddler. Can you even fathom how small that is?"

I narrowed my eyes slightly and tried to picture it. *Not pleasant.*

"There is something that your Changed wife suggested," Sterrin finally relented, grabbing the back of his neck. "She was worried that you would react like this."

"Of course I'm going to react! She is my wife!"

"Please relax, your wife is fine. I have not hurt her; in fact I am much less likely to hurt her at this point than you are, so please calm down."

"Where is she?" I snapped, fingers itching to pluck up the little guy. I would never hurt him, but maybe a little scare would be enough that he would break and tell me where he had hidden Lily. "I swear I will not rest, I will not sleep until I see her. We can't end things this way."

"You had a wonderful moment—"

"*Now.*" I leaned forward, hoping to intimidate without touching. I hated using my size to intimidate this man, but I didn't exactly have anything else. And this wasn't about me. It was about Lily. My Lily. My everything. "What did Lily suggest?"

"Go to your computer," Sterrin said simply.

"Huh?" My eyebrows knotted together.

"You heard me, go to your computer."

I turned my head towards the computer sitting on the desk. Treading carefully, I took a seat in the desk chair. "Okay, now what?"

"Call the number."

"What number . . . come on . . . what's with the riddles?"

"*The number that is on your desk*, you lumbering fool," Sterrin went on, losing patience. "You have Skype; use it."

"Skype?" I realized what he was offering. "You mean—"

"Yes. What is the point of having technology if you can't use it to communicate with the ones you love?"

"Oh my g . . ." I trailed off and quickly set up the microphone and headpiece, dialed the number and waited. My heart swelled, one ring . . . two rings . . . three . . .

"Erik," Lily's voice rang out, clear and full and I let out a trembling breath that I hadn't even realized I was holding.

She was there. Her beauty easily filled the screen before me. Her face suddenly had details again: every freckle, the dimples in her dark cheeks, the dreads of her hair that were slowly coming apart. I didn't have to squint or lean down or pull her close. I could see her.

"Erik, I'm okay," she said with a sad smile.

"How? How did you . . ." I turned around, and Sterrin was gone. *No matter.* I turned my attention back to her. "Lily, I'm so freaking relieved! How are you?" She bit her lip, a motion that I hadn't been able to see clearly in quite a few months.

"Small," she muttered.

"Oh Lily," I whispered, still not used to talking to her in a normal voice. "Are you alright?"

She nodded. "Yes, I'm with Sterrin and Shy."

Jealousy prickled. "Shy?"

Lily smirked. "Sterrin's wife."

"Oh thank God. When I saw you were gone . . . I . . . I almost lost it, Lily. I'm so happy you're safe. That you're okay."

"Me too. And I'm glad I got to see you once more before I say goodbye."

"Goodbye?" My hand started to shake. "It's not goodbye! Lils, don't you see? This way we can still talk, we can wait until you have the rebound effect."

"And if I don't?"

"You will. I know you will. Sterrin thinks so too."

She raised an eyebrow. "Does he?"

"Yes, Lils. I'm not ready to give you up. When you get the rebo—"

"*If* I get it," Lily interjected, but I pressed on.

"When you get it, I'll be everything to you. I'm going to get ready to spend my life with you . . . as a Changed." The word felt so funny on my tongue, but I didn't care. This was Lily. "I don't care what I have to do. I'll learn. I'll start reading books; there must be some sort of the research that I can do—"

"Erik, stories like that aren't real!"

I shook my head. After losing her for just a few hours, I was already so desperate to have her back. I didn't want to think about the things I would do to get her back. "It doesn't matter. They will be real to me. To us. Hell, I bet you got this Skype idea from a story on the internet didn't you?"

Lily blushed. "Misu Pahana used the idea in a story. I thought it made sense so I ran with it."

"Clever girl," I said. "I'll start reading them too. Every day, every moment I'll read them while I wait for you."

"Erik," Lily said slowly. "That could take weeks."

"So it will," I went on. "I'll do it for you, Lily. I'll do anything so we can be together in the end." I reached out and brushed my fingertips on the screen, imagining touching her smooth brown face. Running my fingers through those soft dreadlocks and pressing my mouth against hers. Seeing her on a computer screen, I almost forgot that there was no way I could physically kiss those lips anymore. "Will you promise to wait for me?"

"Who else would I wait for, you big idiot," Lily smiled. "Fine. If this is really something that you want to do."

I nodded. "I do, now tell me what story to try first."

Lily smiled and my heart swelled. *Why did this woman affect me so easily?*

"Well, I suppose you could try this one . . ." She sent the link and I immediately clicked on it.

"*Cole and Ava.*" I read the title out loud. This wasn't going to be easy. Lily's stories always were . . . a little strange. "Alright, I'll do it. I'm going to call you later tonight and tell you my progress.

Will you be there to answer my call?"

"Of course babe, I'll always be there."

I touched her lips on the screen, wishing that I could kiss her. "I'll do my part then. I'll talk to you tonight. Promise?"

"I promise."

She beamed a smile I hadn't seen in weeks.

She would wait for me as long as I could wait for her.

And I could wait until forever.

Fifteen

~ERIK~

I READ. I learned. I did everything I could for Lily during that time.

These were the most crucial times. My parents begged for me to come home, but I worried that if I left that computer, left that cottage, left for more than an hour she would be gone forever. I couldn't afford to make mistakes. Every day I would wake up, take a shower and plop down at the computer and check if Lily was online and available to Skype. If she was, I would sit down and talk to her. She would give me updates until Sterrin or Shy would come along and tell her that they had 'errands.' I tried to gauge how small she was getting by their random appearances, but at that point it didn't matter. Lily was small. Too small to interact directly with me.

Curiosity was a dangerous bitch, always pushing me to ask Lily what these 'errands' were, but Lily said she couldn't talk to an 'Original' about it.

Every time she called me that, it stung a little more.

I tried not to focus on that. This time would pass.

When I wasn't talking with her on Skype I would peruse the internet. Searching for something, anything that I thought might help me be a better husband if Lily could come back to me. I read countless stories, watched the movies, read the books, and scoured the internet. I joined several online communities and even started up a blog called "Tiny-Lives," a written documentary of how I handled my wife's changes. The story was a hit, and people would often comment about how serious I seemed.

"The stories seem so real!" one reader told me in all caps.

"I feel like I am right there with you," said another.

I would smile sadly from behind the computer screen and nod.

An entire subculture was in absolutely in love with my stories.

I started taking polls, asking other fans what they would do to make their loved one feel safer if they were tiny and the responses were always interesting. Apparently I needed to see her as an equal and not be afraid to acknowledge the size differences. I was charmed that so many people took me seriously. Every day I learned a little more: another way to make Lily feel more comfortable, how to hold her, how to 'handle' her, how to speak to her. I wrote down everything. I posted a list entitled "How To Treat a Tiny Woman Right", with collected tips and tricks that I collected.

I was a hero in this new community. I was touched and I would have been happy but for one thing; none of these things seemed to increase the chances of Lily coming back.

One morning I looked at the calendar.

Two months.

Two months had passed since Lily had been taken away from me. Sterrin kept his promise and visited, but it was the 'Originals' in my life who pressured me the most. My parent's patience wore thin.

"I need another month," I said, trying not grow exasperated as my mother questioned me. "She's going to rebound this month."

She sighed over the phone. "That's what you said last month, Erik. And the month before that. I know this is hard, but you have to start making plans. She's not coming back—"

"She's not dead, Mom," I hissed sharply. "I just spoke to her on Skype. She's fine."

Another sigh. "Erik, you can't keep doing this to yourself. Locking yourself up in that cottage, refusing to let anyone visit. It's not healthy. Mark says he can't even reach you. He's afraid to stop by—"

"I can't take the risk. If she comes back, I can't have all these Originals stomping around!"

I was being dramatic, but my fears were warranted. There was no way to be sure if or when Lily was coming back, but no matter what size she was, one 'Original' was enough. I wanted to be the only one who got to see her come back.

"Going on those websites," Mom went on. "You're becoming obsessive. You need to come back home . . . back to reality."

I bristled at her choice of words. "Back to reality? What the hell does that mean? Like Lily isn't real? Like Lily isn't my wife?"

"She was," she began softly.

"*She's my wife*. She's the only woman I'll ever love and the fact that you think that simply because something crazy happened that I can sweep her under the carpet and forget about her? I won't do that! I won't do it!"

"Then when, Erik?"

"When what?"

"You can't see her. You can't be with her. What kind of relationship can you have? You're still so young, and even if this . . . rebound thing you keep talking about—"

"Rebound *effect*," I growled.

"Even if it happens, what then? You want to live your life with a woman only a few inches tall? Is that how you want to live?"

"If it makes her happy—"

"Even if it makes you miserable?"

"*Enough, Mom.* I'm not having this conversation with you."

"I'm want you to be reasonable. What happened to Lily was incredible. And you know we loved her, despite the mistakes she made when she was younger. We took her in, we loved her like she was our own daughter. But now . . . she may not even be that person anymore. She's different, and from what you tell me, she has the chance to live her life with people closer to her own size. Will you really deny her that?"

My retort stuck in the back of my throat. *Could I deny her that?*

"The rebound effect . . ." I stammered, trying to get riled up, already losing my fire.

"How big will she get? Four inches? Five inches? Seven? Does it matter? Do you think either of you will ever feel safe? What if something happens to her? Or to you? Do you think she could live with herself knowing that she is so fully dependent on you?"

The words hurt. Maybe this world wasn't meant for her anymore. I didn't think about what would really happen if she were to live here with me alone. We couldn't go back to the city. And I'd have to go back to work. My grace period was coming to an end. Lily wouldn't want to see any of her old friends or family, and I couldn't stand the idea of leaving her alone in *another* house all day. *Would being together really make her happy? Or just more miserable?* I tried to imagine Lily sitting on the nightstand, alone for hours in a house that wasn't fit for her anymore. I tried to imagine her with only me for company.

I swallowed deeply.

I couldn't be everything to her. No one could truly be everything to one person.

Pressing on to an even more painful idea, I tried to imagine her pain knowing that she could never care for me when I got sick. She could never be the mother of my children. I could never hold her, love her, and kiss her the way that she or I wanted.

Maybe someone else could.

Maybe someone out there could give her a fresh start.

This part of our lives could be a cherished memory, always and forever, and perhaps—and this was a long shot—perhaps we could stay in touch. We could move on with our lives, but still remain close.

"Erik, I can tell that I have given you a lot to think about," Mom said, interrupting my fantasies of hour-long Skype calls where Lily was holding a child in her tattooed arms. A child that wasn't mine. "You're young. She's young. Not all the great loves last forever, but a cherished memory never fades."

"Yes," I answered with a broken voice. "I think I'm beginning to understand what you're saying."

I swear I could hear Mom smiling over the phone. It felt strange, but I felt a sense of relief . . . admitting to myself that maybe this wasn't the end of our lives together, but the beginning of our lives apart. It hurt. It hurt more than words could say, but there was something beautiful about it. A beautiful and painful revelation that could help us both move on into happy and filling lives.

Even if that meant that we couldn't be together.

"I have to go," I told Mom before the tears could come. I wasn't sure if they were tears of joy, relief, or sadness, but I couldn't talk to her anymore.

"I understand, Erik. Will you call me later?" she asked with a worried voice.

"Yes."

"Erik."

"I'll call you after I talk to her, after I explain this to her. I think . . ." the next sentence hurt more than I realized, " . . . I think she will be relieved as well."

"I think so too. I'll talk to you soon."

"I'll talk to you soon, Mom."

There was no going back now. Blinking back tears, I went to the computer and began to close screens. I wrote my final blog entry. I politely excused myself from the forums I joined and began to delete the books I downloaded. They wouldn't be much use to me after my next conversation with Lily. I shut down the computer completely, knowing that the next time I turned it on that I would have to confront Lily. I would have to say good-bye— at least to us ever being together.

I stared at Lily's tiny bed that remained on the nightstand. Walking over, I opened the drawer and swept the bed inside, not quite ready to part with it completely.

And then I picked up the ring that she had once worn and settled it on my pinkie finger.

"I'll get it re-sized," I whispered to the white gold. "I'll wear it forever. Even though it kills me that you can't wear it yourself."

I clenched my fists, suddenly angry. *Why her?*

Collapsing on the bed, the tears came, and I wondered how Lils would spend the rest of her life. Would she re-marry? Would she have the family she always wanted? Would she let them get tattoos like she had? Was such a thing even possible?

My thumb ran across the smoothness of her ring. Lily Larkin would no longer be my wife. Lily Larkin would return to being called Lily Evans and the only people who would even notice were me, my parents and Mark. To everyone else, she was another waitress who got married, left her husband and disappeared off the face of the earth. It wasn't fair.

I buried my face deeper in my arms, dreading the impending conversation that I would have with my wife that night.

With Lily Soon-To-Be-Evans.

It wasn't fair.

Sixteen

~ERIK~

WHEN I FINALLY pulled myself up and checked at the clock, I was shocked to see that it was the next morning. I forgot to Skype with Lily!

Quickly I jumped off the bed, attempted to look somewhat presentable, turned on computer, and quickly dialed the number Sterrin gave to me. I waited, and finally Lily's face filled up the screen.

A gasp escaped my lips.

She was different. Her skin no longer looked dull. Her eyes were brighter and there was a faint blush on her fuller cheeks. I didn't want to admit it, but she also looked like she was either relieved to see me, or flushed from being pulled away from something else. She was happier.

"What's up?" she asked breathlessly. "You okay? You didn't call last night, and I waited for you to show up. You didn't."

My eyes darted around her features, trying to figure out what made her appear so vibrant, as though someone had injected her with a serum full of Technicolor. Had I been so obsessed before that I hadn't noticed that Lily was going through some changes of her own? Her smile was broad, but for some reason, it didn't feel like she was smiling because of me. A horrible pang of jealousy stung my heart as I realized (yet again) that I couldn't be with her. All I wanted was to hold her one last time, even in my hand. I wanted her toned form against my cheek, her dreadlocks entangled in my sloppy, oversized fingertips. I wanted all of these things so badly, but this wasn't why I made the call.

"Erik?" Lily interrupted my thoughts and I brought my attention back to her. "Everything okay?"

I took in a deep breath. Now or never.

"I talked to my mom last night."

Lily raised an eyebrow. "Oh yeah? What does your mom know?" She seemed to be distracted this morning. The conversation with her today felt strained, almost forced . . . but I pressed on.

"You know, the usual. She wants me to come home," I said in a low voice. I stared at Lily through the screen, expecting her to burst out and yell at me to go visit her and that she would be fine, and she would be here when I got back. Instead, she bit her lower lip.

Something was very, very wrong.

"You should go see your family, Erik," Lily said. Her hazel eyes quickly darted towards something behind the screen that I couldn't see.

"Is someone there?" I blurted.

"Erik," she said with a heavy sigh. "I've been doing a lot of thinking . . . and I think you should go home to your family."

"Lils, I don't know how many times I must tell you . . ." My response was so automatic, so used to arguing with her, but Lily interrupted.

"I mean . . . go home permanently," she finished.

We locked eyes through the screen in silence. She had said the exact thing I had come to tell her about. She was at her breaking point as well. There was still some part of me, though, that was upset that she was bringing this up before I did. The smooth metal ring sitting on half of my pinkie felt like lead.

"Why today?" I asked, lowering my head.

"What do you mean?"

"I've been here for over two months now. Why are you telling me this today?"

"It's been on my mind for a while now," she said. "And I think you've been thinking about it as well. We can't live like this."

"What about our promise to always be together?" I asked pathetically, wondering why I was fighting so hard. I had logged on to say goodbye to her, not to beg for her to come back! Still, seeing her face, seeing that strange happiness in her eyes, I felt like I had lost. I had failed as a husband and I was flailing around for that final approval. None of this felt real anymore. Our love. Our relationship. Our marriage. None of it.

"You're right," I finally relented. "We can't do this."

Suddenly, I felt lighter. I was able to look at her, and concede defeat. I loved Lily Larkin—er, Evans. We loved other. We wanted to be together, but the differences were too much now. They were probably too much for anyone and if we ended things now, our love would be something to cherish forever. It was like that horribly depressing movie that Lily always made me watch when she was in a 'girly' mood.

She must have read my mind. "It's like *The Way We Were*," she muttered.

"No it's not." I dared to smile before I fell silent and Lily lowered her eyes.

She wanted to cry; no matter how hard she was, no matter how difficult she could be, she loved me with all of her heart and this was killing her almost as much as it was killing me. One crazy medical condition had rocked our entire lives and now we could no longer be together.

"I would have stayed with you though; I would have been with you if you wanted me to be."

She nodded. "I know that you would. That's what makes this so hard." She sniffed then, the type of sniffing that leads to tears.

I reached out, touched the screen, and caressed her cheek through the computer. "I want to hold you . . . I want to hold you so badly," I couldn't help admitting. "But I can't. You're too small."

"We had ways of getting creative."

"How tall are you now anyways? If you don't mind me asking?"

Lily seemed to mull the question over before responding. "I got it," she whispered as the tears flowed down her coffee colored cheeks.

I leaned forward. "Got what?"

"The rebound effect . . . I got it."

I almost fell out of my seat in shock. "Since when?" I blurted once I was fully composed.

Silence.

"Lils? How long have you had it? And how tall are you now?"

"Does it matter?" she asked.

"Of course it matters! If you come back now—"

Lily shook her head. "No . . . two inches, five inches, or ten inches . . . it's too small. Erik, I can't live in that world anymore. I have to move on . . . I want to move on. Don't you?"

Mom had said the same thing.

"Not without you," I said. "I can't imagine what this world must look like to you now." I swallowed. "What *I* must look like to you now."

"Erik," Lily said softly and I lifted my eyes to meet hers. "You're beautiful. You were then. You are now, and you will be . . . to whoever is lucky enough to snag you."

"I can't even imagine being with another woman," I said. "I spent my whole life looking for someone like you, and now you're slipping through my fingers."

"Literally," Lily tried to joke, but I frowned.

"I know you make jokes when you want to cry, Lily. Won't you come back? Can't I see your face one more time? Not through a computer screen?" I was begging, so desperate to see her once more. I needed to know she was okay. I didn't care how tall she was, I wanted to see her. Touch her. Hold her. Hug her if he could.

When she paused, I pounced.

"Lily, it's the last thing I'll ever ask of you . . . I swear. Please let me see you one more time before we say goodbye."

"And then what will you do?" Lily asked. "I want you go home and try to live a normal life. I want to know that you're married in a few years, with kids, a family—everything you always wanted."

"You're everything I've always wanted. I only wanted those things with *you*," I reminded her. "Lily, please?" My voice cracked and Lily glanced at something behind her. I tried to hide my irritation.

"Give me an hour."

I wondered how she was adjusting to being able to speak normally again. No longer having to shout.

"Really?" I asked.

"Yes. I want to see you one more time as well. Especially now."

I WAITED AT THE WINDOW sill for her. I set up my chair and waited, unsure of what I was looking for. Would she come alone? Would she bring Sterrin? Would Sterrin come along uninvited? I felt strangely large sitting next to the sill. It was only when I started to turn away, when I heard it.

"Erik." A soft voice caressed the air and I spun around.

"Lily," I whispered, immediately lowering my voice to the tone I used with her hours before she was taken away from me. "You look . . ." I trailed off and openly took in her frame. She looked good. Tall. Healthy. Her skin glowed. Her cheeks flushed. Her hair was still in those dreadlocks I loved so much for reasons I could never fully understand.

"Taller?" she asked.

"Yes," I breathed. "H-how tall are you now?"

"Six and a half inches," she said, beaming proudly.

"You have to add the half, don't you?" I forced a grin.

"It's actually not too bad." She flexed a tiny muscle. "I've been climbing with some friends. I'm stronger than I've ever been."

"Friends?" I said, surprised. "You've met others? Like you?" I tried to picture her with others. The thought made my heart ache.

She nodded. "Yes, I live with Shy and Sterrin still, but I'm thinking of changing my arrangements."

The meaning behind the statement took my breath away. *Had she met someone else?*

"Not a guy," Lily said quickly. "I'm still a married woman, remember?"

I cleared his throat. "I'm sorry. I had the most horrible vision."

Lily held out her hand, beckoning me to come closer. I leaned over in my chair towards the sill and Lily's fingertips touched my face. My eyelids felt like they had been set on fire. I never thought I would feel her touch after Sterrin stole her away.

"You need to shave," Lily noted and traced her face down my cheek. "I always say that. And I thought I always would be saying that to you."

"Lily." I barely lifted my voice above a whisper, afraid of jostling her. I was frozen under her touch. She moved and suddenly her tiny cheek pressed against mine. I held in my tears and brought up my hand, cradling her against me. "God, I love you. I always have, and I always will."

She nodded. "I know. I love you too. I can't even imagine life without you."

"It's for the best," I finally agreed.

"It's for the best," she repeated. "That doesn't make it hurt any less."

We fell silent, until she finally let out the tears she needed to shed. She cried hard, the type of crying one couldn't do without support, and as gently as I could, I traced through her hair and down her back with the tip of my finger.

I would never hold her like this again.

"Will I ever get to see you after today?" I dared to ask.

"Do you think we should see each other? It will only make things more difficult. I mean once you're gone, I'm not going to use Skype anymore. It would be too hard for me."

"And me," I relented, hating that all my best laid plans were rejected.

"But . . . but I'll always wonder about you. This is still going to be your parent's cabin, right?"

I pulled my face away slightly, letting Lily fall into the crevice of my palm. She looked so perfect there. So safe. I could have kept her a secret from the world forever if she wanted me to. Even if it meant not seeing my friends or family, I would have done it if she asked. If she needed me that badly.

But she wasn't asking me for that. She didn't need me that badly. She wanted to move on, and despite the pain in my chest, I knew it was the right decision.

"They're going to hold on to this place to rent out when they retire," I muttered.

"There you go. Let's say this . . . in five years."

"Five years?" I blurted, shaking my head. "That's too long."

"Five years to this exact date and time," Lily repeated. "Come back here, and I'll be here. If we want to see each other, we will find each other."

My eyes darted to the calendar. Five years might as well been a lifetime away.

But if that's what she wanted . . .

"Five years then. I'll be back," I said.

Lily, still sitting in my hand, arched her pinkie upward. "Pinky promise?"

"Don't be lame, Lily," I started firmly, unable to stop the chuckle coming through my throat. *Those pinky promises. Would she ever grow up?* I shook my head gently.

No. Lily wouldn't ever grow again.

I held my pinkie out, and she dug her nail into the pad, doing her best to signal the agreement.

"So it's a deal," she said, pulling away. "Five years."

"Five years," I breathed.

Her eyes narrowed towards my hand. "Hey! Are you wearing my wedding band?"

Guiltily, I curled my right hand into a fist. "Uh . . . yeah. I figured someone should."

"Get rid of that thing!" she exclaimed, waving her hand at me. "Sell it back and get some money."

"I don't need money. I want to keep this."

"Erik."

"No arguing. I'm keeping it. Forever. You're not some trinket to throw away."

"People might get the wrong idea."

"To hell with it. You know I don't care what people think."

She suppressed a giggle. "You never did. But . . . but I think I should go," she said slowly, realizing that this truly was the end.

"You don't want to stay? Have some coffee?" I asked pathetically, wondering if I could find her little aluminum foil mug that she had crafted herself.

"No . . ." Lily trailed off, shaking her head. "I *am* a girl after all, babe."

Babe. I wish she hadn't called me that. The familiarity in that term . . . I wasn't ready. "What does that mean?" I asked instead, lowering my face closer to hers. Even at six inches tall, I could see that her eyes were still wet.

"It means I need to go home and cry for a few weeks. Maybe months."

Her voice was so soft that if I wasn't used so straining my ears to hear her, I might not have caught her words. But I did.

"Oh, Lils, are you sure you're going to be okay?" *Was I going to be okay? Was this really the right decision?*

She held it together better than I ever could. "I'll be alright. Will you?"

I lifted my hand towards the sill, and Lily stepped onto it. She turned against my skin and I felt the prickle of her weight all the way into my hair follicles. She was a little surprised when I loomed closer, but when I touched my lips touch to her face she didn't wait for my answer.

I didn't have one anyway.

"Goodbye, Erik," she said quickly.

Her tears seemed to float as she disappeared from my sight.

"Goodbye, Lily."

Five years.

Seventeen

~LILY~

"WHY IS THIS so important to you?" Freddie asked for the umpteenth time as I pulled him along. "I still don't understand why we need to go here today."

"I didn't exactly invite you, did I?" I shot back, with what I hoped was a charming smile.

He flushed without shame.

Freddie was older when he had changed, and still getting used to the Changed lifestyle. After my amazing experience with Sterrin and Sky, I had no problem taking him under my wing when he came into our world. He was six years older than me and for the life of me I didn't understand why he always felt as though he didn't deserve me. He knew I was once married to an Original and had stayed with him as long as I could, but I didn't tell him much more than that.

Erik Larkin was my 'cherished memory', and Freddie was okay with that.

BUT EVERYTHING HAD CHANGED YESTERDAY morning when I checked my handmade calendar and realized with a mixture of surprise and horror that nearly five years had passed since my 'cherished memory'.

"Has it really been five years already?"

I heard the slight padding behind me as Freddie stood on his tiptoes to rest his chin on my shoulder. I was taller than him, another thing that I never had to get used to with Erik, which was easy to get used to. I was taller than most guys I knew before I had changed so, in a way, I was back into familiar territory.

"Five years since what?" Freddie asked.

"Five years since my ex-husband and I decided we couldn't be together. We promised to meet after five years . . . I wonder if he even remembers." I shook my head, and stepped away. "Probably not, I'm sure he's married with kids and who knows what else." Even after all this time, the idea of Erik holding another woman made my stomach stir.

"Well . . . Lily, it's not like you haven't been busy," Freddie muttered.

I smiled down at the tiny bundle in his strong, squared hands.

"Yes I know, Kara is everything to me," I said affectionately, taking the baby away from him. "It will be weird, I suppose—to see him."

"When is the exact day?" Freddie asked, smiling fondly and shifting uncomfortably at the same time.

"Tomorrow."

Never before had I looked forward to and dreaded a day so much.

"SO THIS IS THE PLACE?" Freddie asked as we stood under an untended hedge in front of a house that didn't seem to have any residents. It was still the same sad cabin in the woods.

I nodded. "This is it. Where happiness comes to die."

"You don't have to make it sound so morbid."

I smiled. "You're right, and yes, his parents let us use it once I was too small to . . . too small," I said, noting the empty driveway and drawn curtains. Maybe he had forgotten. Freddie took my hand in his.

"He'll be here," he said softly. "No man would be able to forget you."

"Yeah right," I chortled.

"Have you looked at you lately?" he teased.

I laughed as my cheeks blazed crimson. Freddie was so freaking adorable that it hurt sometimes.

"Look!" Freddie called out suddenly and my eyes darted towards the house.

A car was coming up the dirt driveway. A newer, fancier-looking car than I remembered, but I knew in my heart that this car belonged to him.

Would he be alone? Would he have a wife? Would he have children?

"Maybe we should go," I whispered, trying to pull away. I wasn't so sure what I was afraid of, but Freddie held on tight to my hand, refusing to let me escape.

"No, you said that you wanted to see him."

"Yes, and now I'm sure that I don't."

"Don't be ridiculous. You are going to stand right here and at least . . . *Look!* It's stopping."

So it was him. He had remembered. He had come. My lips parted with unspoken anxiety as I waited and strained to hear voices.

There was more than one.

A female voice.

A child. Maybe more than one of those as well.

"Dad!" someone whined out suddenly. His youthful cry filled the air. "Why do we have to come *here?*"

"Yeah, Dad," a female voice added in.

"Tyler, Cherish," an older female voice chided the other two younger voices. "That's enough. Your father wanted to come here and we wanted to do so as a family. This place means something to you, doesn't it, sweetie?"

Sweetie. That word always churned in my stomach. I would have never called him that, but I also couldn't hide my approval when the owner of the voice exited the car. She was tiny, soft, and elegant with chestnut brown hair and eyes only a slightly dark shade of blue than Erik's. I hadn't expected her to be a young and beautiful looking housewife. Even better, she had a gentle expression. I smiled gently as the woman took the girl child up into her arms, kissing both her cheeks.

"Can you be a good girl for Daddy?" she asked the child who smirked back at her.

"For Daddy," she laughed.

"And Tyler? Can you behave for Daddy?"

"No! I don't want—"

"Oh, leave him be."

A deep voice rumbled out then and my heart nearly exploded from my chest.

Erik.

His familiar shape stepped out of the car, clad in a blue polo and khaki shorts. His face was clean-shaven, and though his sunglasses looked expensive, even from a distance it was obvious that he was still cutting his own hair.

He was still him.

"He's married," I whispered as his new family got situated.

Something pushed me forward. "Well . . ." Freddie urged gently.

"Well what?" I stammered. "I just . . . I just needed to see that he's okay . . ."

"Go talk to him!"

My cheeks reddened. "I can't just walk up! He has kids! And a wife! And I," I turned to Freddie. "I have a husband. We have our own lives now," I trailed off then as something flashed in the sun and spun back around to face my ex-husband.

The ring. It was on his pinky now, just as he promised it would always be.

"I don't believe him," I couldn't help whispering. "The goof."

"You guys go inside and get everything set up." Erik's voice rumbled to the rest of the group. "There's something I have to take care of. I'll be in in a few minutes."

"Dad . . ." the boy whined.

"Tyler . . . enough," Erik said and allowed the woman to pull his family away. It seemed as though the two were sharing a moment, their eyes met and she whispered 'go ahead'.

Freddie's hand left mine.

"What are you doing?" I asked, not turning to look at him. I couldn't tear my gaze away from Erik. I felt ashamed, but not enough so to turn away. Had it really been five years?

"This is a private moment. Between you and him. I understand that."

My expression softened. "Why are you so good to me?"

"Go."

"Lils?" Erik's voice called out quietly once his family was inside. "Lils? Are you out here?"

Freddie pushed me forward. "I'm good to you because I worship the ground you walk on. Enough so that I'm sending you out to speak to your ex who looks like someone out of a *GQ* magazine. So go. Talk to him." He softly kissed my cheek. "I'll be back at the house with Kara and Shy."

I turned away and watched him go, feeling more and more

nervous as he disappeared into the grass. Erik was still carefully rummaging around in the clearing and calling my name. He kept his eyes locked on the ground.

Five years. Five years had passed and now we both had our own lives.

A wife. A husband. Three children between the two of us.

"Lils," Erik whispered, and finally I gathered up my courage.

"Eri!" I called, watching his features soften. He sought out my voice for only a moment before his eyes landed on me.

I stepped towards him. He stepped towards me. Like moths to a flame, we would always be drawn to one another. We were kindred spirits and not even five years apart and over six feet of height difference could change that.

When we were close enough, Erik slowly lowered himself into a crouching position, using his hand to support himself. The ring which symbolized our marriage glinted in the sunlight and his eyes watered. Mine did the same as the memories of our previous life together all came flooding back at once. That feeling of familiarity and safety. But it wasn't the same type of love. It was more.

I drew closer, and reached out to touch his pant leg and arched my head back to meet those familiar ice blue eyes which always warmed my heart.

"Hi, Erik." A sad smile filled with longing must have crossed my face because Erik returned a mirrored expression.

My knees began to give out.

"Hello, Lily."

We both fell silent, unsure of where to start.

If you liked this book,
And I really hope you do
Please write your review!

About the Author

C.E. WILSON IS currently living in Pittsburgh, Pennsylvania with her husband, beautiful daughter, fat beagle and two cats. They are all the loves of her life. She loves horror movies and shoujo manga. When it rains she feels at peace and loves a sweet cup of coffee with way too much sugar and cream. She loves the fall because of football and all things pumpkin. Her favorite subject to write about is size difference, but she enjoys to try her hand at all things fantastical.

www.cewilsonauthor.com

Sign up for my Newsletter to find out the

latest news and apply for free goodies!!

www.facebook.com/cewilsonauthor

www.goodreads.com/CEWilson

twitter.com/cewilson1

www.instagram.com/cewilsonauthor

Other titles by

C.E. WILSON

STANDALONE NOVELS

This is Me.

To Nowhere

The Boy with Words

THE PUNISHMENT SERIES

COMING SOON FROM C.E.

Untitled Beauty (Fall 2016)

Cruel and Unusual (Winter 2016)

A Death's Awakening (2017)

Playing Human (2017)

Made in the USA
Charleston, SC
01 September 2016